Hide and Seek

by Peter Lerangis

AN
APPLE
PAPERBACK

SCHOLASTIC INC.
New York   Toronto   London   Auckland   Sydney
Mexico City   New Delhi   Hong Kong   Buenos Aires

Many thanks to Robert Leighton,
co-founder of the amazing
puzzability.com, for his
technical help with this book
and, moreover, his friendship.

ISBN 0-439-50726-X

Text copyright © 2004 by Peter Lerangis.

All rights reserved. Published by Scholastic Inc.
SCHOLASTIC, APPLE PAPERBACKS, and associated logos are trademarks
and/or registered trademarks of Scholastic Inc.

Design by Joyce White

12 11 10 9 8 7 6 5 4 3 2 1   4 5 6 7 8 9/0
                                                  40
Printed in the U.S.A.
First printing, October 2004

Prologue

Mom was gone.

Forever.

Andrew tried to fight the idea. But it haunted him.

Sure, she'd contacted them once. Back in Connecticut. But it had taken her *ten months* to do that. And she'd had the help of a tough old spy, whose code name was Foxglove.

But Foxglove had been discovered. Which meant that Mom may have been discovered, too.

That was the worst part. The uncertainty.

The other worst part was that even if Mom *was* okay, even if she wanted to get back in touch with him and Evie and Pop, they weren't in Connecticut anymore.

When your dad works in covert military operations, you move around. A lot. Often without leaving a trace, and at a moment's notice.

Andrew tossed his duffle bag on the bed as his twin sister barged into the room. "Make sure the movers didn't steal Mom's stuff — what's left of it," Evie said, dumping a box marked SAN FRANCISCO MOVERS on the mattress. "And don't mope."

"I'm not moping," Andrew replied.

"Mom will find us." Evie turned to leave. "She has ways."

Evie could read his mind. It was one of her most annoying traits. She considered herself older, smarter, and more mature than Andrew. Only one of those things was true. On November 11 at 3:43 A.M. she would be exactly twelve years old. Andrew wouldn't turn twelve until 3:47. Evie was four minutes older.

To Evie, those four minutes counted for a lot.

Two moving men clomped by Andrew's open door, followed by his dad, who stopped for a moment to gaze out Andrew's window. "Best view in the house," he proclaimed.

In the afternoon light, the red-orange spires of the Golden Gate Bridge peeked over the rooftops. San Francisco was a cool place. It had steep hills, cable cars, and a chocolate factory within walking distance of their new house.

But it was three thousand miles from Connecticut.

And a universe away from Mom.

Andrew tore open the box and removed pajamas, sweaters, and a spiral notebook. Hidden underneath was an envelope that contained all the stuff Mom had sent them. From wherever she was. Carefully he opened it and examined the contents: one universal key that opened all locks; one typewritten story, in code; one sheet of paper with the hidden message decoded.

There had been one more thing. It looked like a child's kaleidoscope, but it was actually a high-powered telescope that doubled as a camera. That was gone now. Andrew had searched their Connecticut house high and low, but he'd somehow lost it — a fact Evie kept reminding him about during the trip. That was another one of her annoying traits. She never forgot a single one of his mistakes.

Andrew unfolded the sheet of paper on which he and Evie had solved the code. Even though he'd memorized it and analyzed it a million times, it remained a mystery:

> Dear ones: I am a spy. Cannot tell you where I am. Need your help. Foxglove will assist you. Be careful. Tell no one, not even Father. Expect another parcel. Don't worry, we'll be together soon. I love you. Spy X.

Spy X?

What kind of code name was that for a *mom?*

Who could she be spying for? Who was she hiding from?

And why did she leave when she did — on 11 11 11, the eleventh day of the eleventh month last year, when Evie and Andrew turned eleven?

Ever since they were little kids, they'd looked forward to that day because it was such a cool set of numbers. It almost seemed like a code itself. But now they didn't want to remember it.

Andrew reached under the pile of clothes in the box and took out another envelope. From it he removed an old photo of himself and Mom at his preschool street fair. They had stuck their heads through a life-size wooden cutout of a comic-strip scene. Andrew was a buff Superman, swooping down from the open sky. Mom was Lois Lane, plunging downward from the top of a skyscraper. Her eyes were wide in an expression of mock horror. In the picture, Andrew was smiling broadly, with all the strength and confidence of a four-year-old. He remembered thinking how funny it was — *Mom* had always done the rescuing, always been the one to make things turn out right. He loved the feeling of rescuing her. And he remembered taking it for granted that if he had to, he would.

He smiled, tucking the photo away in his new dresser.

Sometimes, when he looked at it, he still had that feeling.

Chapter One

"Evie, he's *flirting*," Andrew whispered, gesturing toward the sidewalk.

Evie looked over her shoulder, through the open gate of Adolph Green Middle School. Pop, who had just driven them to their first day of school, was chatting with another parent. "He is *talking*," Evie said. "It's called being social. Pop is not a babe magnet, Andrew. Besides, he's already married, *and so is she*!"

"I just don't like it," Andrew replied.

He turned into the playground, holding a black metallic device that was connected to his ears via a long wire.

His Star Raiders Intergalactic Cell Communicator.

This morning he was Galactic Commander Anakin Wall-P-5-Q-2, on a Mission to Save the Earth from Shape-Changing Spies. Evie didn't mind this role as much as his other favorite — Bombardier A. Wall, World War II Flying Ace, Making the Town Safe for Humanity.

Whenever they moved, it took Andrew awhile to make his debut as just-plain Andrew. Evie had learned to be patient. Sort of.

Mom used to say the world was divided into two kinds of people: those who looked at half a glass of water and said it was half full, and those who said it was half empty. Andrew was a third type. He'd spill the water and tell you it would have evaporated anyway.

To Andrew, life was always a battle with the Dark Side. As a baby he'd arrange his Pampers like an invading army, then vanquish them with his milk bottle. His favorite hobby, even now, was riding his bike for hours, pretending to be in a plane or space vessel. Reality was his biggest enemy. It made him nervous. He hated meeting people. Which was a problem when you had to move a lot.

Evie understood all of this. She loved her brother and usually left him to his imagination. But jumping into a new school on a Wednesday of the third week of classes was stressful enough, and her patience was running out.

They turned a corner of the building, where people were gathered around two card tables. School election posters had been taped to the walls behind the tables.

A curly-haired girl with glasses smiled at Andrew. "Hi, I'm Rosie, who are you?"

"Anakin," Andrew replied.

Evie groaned. "He means Andrew. It's a speech impediment. I'm Evie. We're new."

"Doreen, newbies!" Rosie shouted over her shoulder.

A girl came out from behind the table, her blond ringlets bouncing as if they had a life of their own. She wore a crisp white cotton sweater, a pleated plaid skirt, and a smile right out of a toothpaste ad. "Welcome!" she squealed, thrusting flyers at Andrew and Evie. "You *have* to vote for me, Doreen Franklin, for student council president. I promise to form an official welcoming committee for new students, with mandatory milk and cookies."

"Cool," Andrew said.

Doreen smiled. "He's cute," she said, winking at Evie.

Andrew began turning shades of red. As Doreen went back to the table, Evie glanced at the flyer. It was a huge photo of Doreen surrounded by a red, white, and blue logo: VOTE FOR DOREEN, THE BEST EVER SEEN, FOR PRESIDENT OF ADOLPH GREEN!

"I'm cute?" Andrew said. "Really?"

Evie folded the paper and put it into her pocket. "At least until the election."

They walked through a courtyard into a whitewashed building with high, curved arches and mosaic tile floors. The kids in San Francisco walked faster and talked faster than they did in Shoreport, Connecticut. They looked different, too. On her way to homeroom, Evie counted twenty-one kids with body piercings, a girl with hair in three colors and three different lengths, a boy in a kilt, and a group of students who seemed to have taken fashion cues from Edward Scissorhands.

City kids, Evie decided, were just *different*.

Homeroom was in a carpeted room with a jazz CD playing. After giving Andrew and Evie their locker assignments, the teacher, Mr. Xing, threw a small party for them. The class sat in a big circle, eating muffins and chocolate croissants.

Afterward, Andrew and Evie rushed to their lockers, which were in a hallway near the gym.

"I've decided this is the last move," Evie exclaimed, pulling a lock out of her backpack. "I want to live here forever."

Andrew squinted at his locker assignment. "I'd like it better if someone hadn't stolen my locker."

Evie checked her number, 1106. The locker was open and empty.

Andrew's, number 1107, was shut tight. A heavy-duty padlock hung from the handle, with a shank so thick it barely fit through the hole.

"Let's tell Mr. Xing," Evie said.

"No need." Andrew dug into his pockets and pulled out the special key that Mom had sent them. The one that opened any lock.

"Andrew, be real," Evie said. "That lock doesn't belong to you."

"So? It's my *locker,* isn't it?" With his fingernail, Andrew slowly turned the ridges that surrounded the key's head. The key's teeth moved, retracting inward, making the key thinner. He inserted the key into the lock and carefully turned it. He could feel the teeth working their way down inside the lock, fitting the tumblers.

With a satisfying *snap*, the lock fell open. Andrew pulled it off, and the locker door swung out. The walls were dented and rusty, the hooks empty. A battered old wooden crate sat on the top shelf.

"Oh, great, what am I supposed to do with this?" Andrew asked, pulling the crate out.

Through the crate's slats, Evie could see someone's sneaker. Pink and orange. On top was a small label, covered with scribbled initials. Nothing in recognizable English. She glanced at the clock. One minute to class. "Leave it for now, Andrew. We'll find a lost-and-found later."

Andrew ignored her. He set the crate on the floor, lifted off the top, and pulled out the pink-and-orange sneaker — a brand-new Converse low-top basketball shoe for the right foot. Size seven, Andrew's size. Tucked inside was something metallic and white.

An iPod.

"All *riiiiight*!" Andrew said.

"Hello? Can you spell 'juvenile court'?" Evie calmly took the sneaker and iPod away from him, setting them in the crate with all the other things — a set of silver binoculars, a cassette player, a folded-up sheet of graph paper, a crumpled-up envelope, and a rubber-gripped metal handle etched with PROPERTY OF SFCCM / 817543962.

As she lifted the top, she caught a glimpse of the label.

N D N E
D A A I
R W V L
W E L E

Odd.

It reminded her of a Boggle game. She loved re-arranging Boggle cubes, trying to make words out of the random letter combinations.

Right away she saw EVIL and WELL and WARD and NAVEL and . . .

She brought the paper closer, barely noticing the sharp clanging of the start-of-period bell.

Andrew snatched back the iPod. "Finders keepers," he grumbled, inserting its headphones into his ears.

"Andrew?" Evie said. "Look at this!"

With a sudden scream, Andrew yanked the earplugs out. "Your voice — it came through the iPod!"

"You downloaded my voice?"

"No! There's something wrong with this. It's like a microphone or something. It's picking you up."

"That's weird . . ." Evie said. "And speaking of weird, what does this remind you of?" She turned the label so Andrew could see it.

"The chart at the eye doctor?"

"No! *Boggle!*"

Andrew made a face. "I hate Boggle."

"That's because I always win."

With her finger, she traced out a connected E, V, I, E.

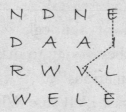

"Congrats," Andrew said. "Can we go to class now?"

"You're in there, too, Andrew," she said. She took out a pen from her pack, placed it at the lower right-hand corner, and began connecting letter to letter. This time she didn't stop at her own name:

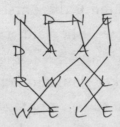

" 'Evie . . . and . . . Andrew . . . Wall'?" Andrew murmured.

Evie's face was tense with excitement. "It's Mom," she said. "She found us. I knew she would. She *told* us to expect another package — and here it is!"

"But . . . a sneaker?" Andrew said, sifting through the junk in the crate. "A defective iPod?"

"A microphone, binoculars — *spy stuff*, Andrew."

"But any normal kid could have those things," Andrew said. "Look, it doesn't make sense that this came from Mom. We didn't even tell anyone we were moving.

How could she know we were here? How could she figure out what school we were going to *and* which lockers were ours — and then put a crate together, sneak into the school, and leave it for us?"

Evie took a deep breath. For once, *she* was the one clinging to a fantasy.

She folded the label and put it into her pocket. They were now officially late for their first-period class. "Lock up that crate, Andrew," she said, turning to go. "Let's book."

She heard the locker slam shut and the lock click into place. Andrew ran up to her, ripping open an envelope.

"What are you doing?" she asked.

"It fell out of the crate. There's something inside." A black stone fell into his hand — a jewel, polished and shiny.

Just ahead of them, the door to their first-period class slammed shut. "Great, Andrew, just great! Brand-new in the school, and we've already broken into a locker, been late for our first class, and stolen a jewel! We might as well put up WANTED photos of ourselves in the post office!"

Andrew was unfolding a note he'd found inside the envelope. He flattened it out on the classroom door:

1-23-1-32

HSVZŔBKNRḊZLEHMD

NCĊMEQ̇PHKḞGPĖGVQIKXGEṄẄGU

LQEḂOJBXKPKBZḂPPXOV

WBSJ̇PVṪMPDBUJ̇PȮT

HDJOHYXOWXUHMDFNDO

SLḞYLBQRMLCRṀPYCQSTCL

ZYAIĊBSNJCDR

Evie's hand froze on the doorknob.
The handwriting was unmistakable.
Andrew smiled. "It's Mom. You win."

Chapter Two

One, twenty-three, one, thirty-two . . .

Andrew entered the numbers on his PDA. Adolph Green Middle School had wireless Web access, and his math teacher had given him a link to a site that analyzed numerical patterns. As he walked toward the cafeteria, he was oblivious to the swarm of kids around him.

All that mattered was Mom's code.

He and Evie had learned something about professional codes back in Connecticut. You looked for a key first — some sort of clue that showed you how to solve the code.

He figured the numbers on top of Mom's note — 1-23-1-32 — were the key to this code. But what did they mean?

INSUFFICIENT DATA TO DETERMINE SEQUENCE, the screen answered back. CHECK IF DIGITS ARE PROPERLY ENTERED.

"Rats," Andrew said under his breath.

Lousy site. There had to be another one. As he entered the cafeteria, he furiously thumbed the URL of another search engine.

And he ran smack into someone just inside the door.

"Klutz," said Doreen Franklin, spinning around to face him.

"Ooops . . ." Andrew squeaked.

"Try 'I'm sorry.' It's called manners." Doreen smiled stiffly. "Have a nice lunch. And vote Doreen for Adolph Green!"

"Um . . ." Andrew said, but he couldn't muster another syllable.

Rushing into the cafeteria from behind him, Evie took Andrew by the arm. "Did you crack the code key?"

"No. And I don't think Doreen finds me cute anymore."

"We'll have to postpone the wedding." Evie pulled Andrew toward the back of the cafeteria. A perky girl ran up and handed them each a button. The buttons had her picture on them, along with the words A VOTE FOR YU IS A VOTE FOR YOU!

Evie shoved the button into her pocket and pushed open the back door that led outside. "We can't let *anyone* see us with the code. You never know who is spying."

Andrew looked longingly at the lunch line. "But they're having liverwurst today. I love liverwurst."

They ducked behind a row of thick bushes that lined the brick wall. "Now," Evie said. "The message is pretty long, lots of letters. So I thought the numbers might mean, 'Go one letter, then skip twenty-three, go one more, then go thirty-two . . .'" She sighed. "So I tried it, but all I got was gibberish."

Andrew scratched his head. "I wonder if this is a message at all. I mean, it's just six lines with six strings of letters — no spaces, no punctuation, nothing."

"What about those dots?"

"A leaky pen, maybe? I don't know. It's weird. Four numbers. Six lines. Dots. No words."

He glanced at the message, still on the screen of his PDA: CHECK IF DIGITS ARE PROPERLY ENTERED.

One again he looked at Mom's writing:

1-23-1-32

He knew the numbers were entered right.

But digits?

"Evie?" Andrew said. "Is there a difference between numbers and digits?"

Evie raised an eyebrow. "I guess you must have been absent that day in second grade. Yeah, there is. Like, *twelve* is one number, but it has two digits — *one* and *two*."

Taking a pen from his pocket, Andrew began carefully drawing vertical lines:

1|-2|3|-1|-3|2

"So these are the digits?" he said. "Plus one, minus two, plus three, minus one, minus three, plus two?"

"Yes. So?"

"Six digits, six lines. One digit for each line. It might be a clue."

With his pen, Andrew drew the six digits in order along the left side of the note:

```
      1|-2|3|-1|-3|2
  +1  HSVZŘBKNRDZLEHMD
  −2  NCÉMEQ̇PHKFGPÉGVQIKXGEŃWGU
  +3  LQEBOJBXKPKBZBPPXOV
  −1  WBSJPVTMPDBUJPOT
  −3  HDJOHYXOWXUHMDFNDO
  +2  SLFYLBQRMLCRMPYCQSTCL
      ZYAICBSNJCDR
```

"What could that *mean*?" Evie asked.

"I was hoping you'd know," Andrew said.

"Maybe it's something to do with the alphabet. Like, you decode the first line by adding *one* to each letter. A is really B, C is really D, and so on."

Andrew nodded. "So on the first line, you'd replace H with the next letter, I. And S would go to T, V to W . . . what about the Z?" Andrew asked.

"Back to A, I guess."

Andrew began writing:

+1 HSVZRBKNRDZLEHMD
ITWASCLOSEAMFINE

" 'It was close. Am fine.' " Evie nearly jumped out of the bushes. "She's okay! Andrew, you're a genius!"

"Well, maybe just a little gifted," Andrew said modestly, squinting at the note. "Okay. The next line is a minus two — each letter goes two letters back. So, like, Z would be . . . X!"

"And D would be B," Evie said. "B would go back to Z, A to Y . . ."

It took a long time and involved a lot of erasing, but slowly they transcribed each line:

+1 HSVZŘBKNRĎZLEHMD
ITWASCLOSEAMFINE

−2 NCĚMEQ̇PHKFGPĚGVQIKXGEŇWGU
LACKCONFIDENCETOGIVECLUES

+3 LQEBOJBXKPKBZBPPXOV
OTHERMEANSNECESSARY

−1 WBSJPVTMPDBUJPOT
VARIOUSLOCATIONS

−3 HDJOHYXOWXUHMDFNDO
EAGLEVULTUREJACKAL

+2 SLFYLBQRMLCRMPYCQSTCL
UNHANDSTONETORAESUVEN

ZYAIČBSNJCDR
BACKEDUPLEFT

"'It was close,'" Andrew read. "'Am fine. Lack confidence to give clues. Other means necessary . . .'"

"Other means? What's she talking about?" Evie asked.

"Different kinds of clues, maybe," Andrew said. "Smoke signals. E-mail. I don't know. What I don't get is 'various locations.' Does she want us to go to other places?"

"The zoo, maybe?" Evie guessed. "That's where you find an eagle, a vulture, and a jackal."

"Mom hates the zoo. All those poor trapped animals . . ."

They both stared at the last line. The most confusing of all.

Unhand stone to raesuven backed up left.

"The stone must be the black stone," Andrew said. "I guess we have to unhand it. Give it to somebody. But who's Rae Suven?"

"Sounds like a nonsense word to me," Evie replied. "Remember what Mrs. D taught us about word puzzles? Some of the clues contain hints — like, if it says 'mixed up' you have to mix letters up —"

"Right. And *backed up* could mean reading a word backward!"

"What's *Rae Suven* backward?" Evie asked.

Andrew carefully spelled it out on the side of Mom's note.

NEVUSEAR.

"Well, *that* sure helps," Evie said dryly.

But Andrew was already at his PDA, typing the word NEVUS into an online dictionary.

With a sudden smack of the metal handle, the cafeteria door swung open. "Duck!" Evie whispered, pulling Andrew down behind the bush.

Doreen and Rosie stepped out of the cafeteria. Looking quickly in both directions, they scurried over near a Dumpster against the wall on the opposite side of the door.

"Give me the iPod!" Evie whispered.

Andrew handed it to her. She put the phones in her ears and pointed the device in the girls' direction.

"Did you see what Sarah Yu is giving out?" came Doreen's voice, loud and clear. "*Buttons!*"

"She's so conceited," Rosie replied.

"She's brilliant," Doreen said. "Why didn't *you* think of that? What kind of campaign manager are you? *Everybody's* wearing those buttons. If each button translates into one vote, she'll win!"

Evie peeked through the leaves of the bush.

Doreen was pacing by the Dumpster. Rosie was red-faced and overwhelmed. Adjusting her glasses, she said, "Um . . . I could find out how to order them —"

"Not enough time," Doreen shot back. "We're over. Done. This is humiliating. The kids are going to cast their ballots, and Sarah's name is going to be announced over the loudspeaker — for the whole school to hear! *And it's all your fault.*"

"Not necessarily . . ." Rosie said meekly.

"We only have two *days*," Doreen said. "Do you have some *miracle* in mind?"

"If we can't do anything *before* the vote," Rosie said with a sly smile, "we still have *after*. Once the ballots are in — well, a ballot is just a little slip of paper, you know. We could make a few of them ourselves — like *beforehand* . . ."

"I don't believe this," Evie whispered. "They're going to rig the election."

But Andrew was watching the screen of his PDA come to life. "Evie!" he said. "Nevus means *mole*!"

"Let me see that." Evie grabbed the PDA. "We're supposed to give the black stone to a *mole*?"

Andrew replaced the words "raesuven back up" with "ear mole" and read aloud: "'Unhand stone to . . . ear mole on left'? That doesn't make sense."

The bushes suddenly parted. "*What do you think you're doing?*"

"Agggh!" Evie yanked the earphones from her ears.

Doreen and Rosie were standing over them. Both girls had their arms folded.

Andrew stared back, frozen.

"Simon says . . . 'Speak,'" Doreen hissed.

"Just having a little, uh, twin time," Evie replied. "Right, Andrew?"

Andrew didn't reply. He was staring at Doreen's left ear.

Just above her earring was a large, purplish mole.

Chapter Three

"Here, Doreen," Andrew said, reaching into his pocket. "This is for you."

He pulled out the black stone and thrust it toward her.

Evie leaped up. "What are you doing, Andrew?"

Too late. Doreen was turning the stone over in her hand, examining it.

"Give it back!" Evie blurted out. "He didn't mean to do that. You see, ever since you called him cute, he's lost his mind —"

"I *did* mean to," Andrew protested, then lowered his voice to a whisper. "Rae suven," he hissed, his eyes darting toward Doreen. "Nevus ear!"

Rosie glared at him. "You guys are foreigners?"

"See what I mean, he's talking nonsense," Evie said. "He can't be held accountable for his stupid actions."

Andrew mouthed the word *mole*, pointed to his left ear, then pointed at Doreen.

Evie saw it. A mole near the left earring.

Could that really be it? They were supposed to give the precious stone to *her*?

"Do you know what this stone is?" Doreen asked, looking intently at Andrew.

"Asteroidal blackstone," Andrew improvised. "From a meteor that fell in the South Nebraskan desert. I hear it's radioactive."

Doreen pulled a hanky out of her pocket, wrapped the stone in it, and put it in her pocket. "I could have sworn it was onyx. Let's go, Rosie."

As she stepped inside, Rosie lingered behind. She fiddled nervously with the ends of her hair. "You guys didn't happen to hear Doreen and me talking, did you?"

"Talking?" Andrew said. "You were talking?"

"A planning session," Rosie said. "For our new administration. You *are* voting, right?"

"If she doesn't give back the stone, I'm voting for Yu," Evie said.

Rosie gave her a puzzled look. "I'm not running."

"Not you," Andrew said, giggling. "Yu. Who's on first? What's on second?"

"What?" Rosie said.

"Yes. And I Don't Know's on third!" Andrew looked hopefully into Rosie's vacant eyes. "It's a comedy skit? Abbott and Costello?"

The class bell rang, and Evie grabbed her brother by the arm before he could do any more damage.

Andrew carried the crate in front of him as he and Evie walked home after school. "Asteroidal blackstone from the South Nebraskan desert . . . who's on first . . ." Evie grumbled. "There *is* no desert in Nebraska. Abbott and Costello are dead. And you shouldn't have given that stone to her!"

"She had the mole, Evie!"

"A lot of people have moles. Spies don't jump to conclusions! Mom's hiding, people are after her, and she needs us. Do you really think her first clue would be to give a jewel to *Doreen*? What asteroidal stone is your head made of?"

"Okay, okay, so we'll get it back," Andrew said. "We'll offer her something better in return."

"Like what?"

"A diamond?"

"She'll think you're proposing."

"Ha-ha." Andrew made a face at his sister and then glanced behind them. "Okay, we're, like, miles away from school. Can we look inside the crate now?"

Evie looked over her shoulder. They were four blocks away from school, just over a steep hill. She could see no students. No one who would snoop. "Okay. Let's see Mom's note again."

Andrew set the crate down. He gave Evie the note and began rummaging around the other stuff.

"Andrew?" Evie said. "These dots — over the letters — I'm not sure they're a mistake. I think the letters under the dots spell something."

Andrew looked over her shoulder. "R, D, E, Q . . . ?"

+1 HSVZŔBKNRĎZLEHMD
ITWASCLOSERMFINE

−2 NCEMEQ̇ṖHKḞGPĖGVQ̇IKXGEŃẄGU
LACKCONFIDENCETOGIVECLUES

+3 LQEḂOJBXKPKBZBPPXOV
OTHERMEANSNECESSARY

−1 WBSJPVṪMPDBUJPȮṪ
VARIOUSLOCATIONS

−3 HDJOHYXOWXUHMDFNDO
EAGLEVULTUREJACKAL

+2 SLFYLBQRMLCRMPYCQSTCL
UNHANDSTONETORRESUVEN

ZYAIĊBSNJCDR
BACKEDUPLEFT

"Not those letters," Evie said. "The *decoded* ones — *under* the dotted letters!"

Andrew tried again. "S, E, C, O, N, D, C, L, U, E, I, S, I, N, S, H, O, E . . ."

"That's it," Evie said. "The second clue is in shoe!"

"Something *was* in the shoe. The iPod with the mike."

Evie took the iPod from her pocket and examined it. There were no songs loaded into it, no secret messages written on it. "Was there something else in there?" She knelt down, removed the sneaker from the box, and turned it upside down.

Two newspaper clippings fell out. One was an ad for a DVD of a movie, *My Left Foot*. The other was a tag that said Van Ness Shoes.

"My left foot . . . Van Ness Shoes . . ." Andrew muttered. "But this shoe belongs to a *right* foot."

"It makes perfect sense," Evie said.

"It does?"

"The shoe is missing its mate. Mom wants us to find it. We need to get the left sneaker — at Van Ness Shoes!"

"Why would Mom want us to get a shoe?" Andrew asked.

Evie pointed to Mom's note. "Look what this says — 'Lack confidence to give clues. Other means necessary.

Various locations.' She needs us to go to another location to find this. Maybe there's a secret message inside. Or maybe you're supposed to wear it for some reason. It could be a signal to someone — another helper, somebody like Mrs. Digitalis."

"So Mom's sending us on a scavenger hunt," Andrew said.

"That's it, Andrew!" Evie blurted out. "The fifth line — you've figured it out! 'Eagle, vulture, jackal' — they do have something in common. They're *scavengers*."

A cable car's bell resounded behind them. It was climbing the hill, its wheels whirring on the track beneath.

"Mom is always so protective," Andrew said. "Why would she do this — make us run all over the city?"

Evie swallowed hard. Her eyes welled up. "Andrew . . . read the first letter of each line. Go ahead."

Andrew took the note. "I . . . love . . . u."

It was Mom, all right. And she wouldn't send them on this mission unless she had to.

Andrew threw the shoe in the crate, tucked it under his arm, and ran toward the cable car stop. "Come on! The driver will tell us how to get to Van Ness Shoes."

"We can't do that!" Evie said. "Pop made us promise not to travel in the city all by ourselves."

Andrew turned. "What else can we do? We can't ask him to take us. We'd have to tell him why."

Evie knew he was right. Mom had made it clear in her first note — the one she'd sent them in Connecticut — that Pop was not to know a thing. He couldn't know that she was in touch at all. She was shielding him for some reason. If they were going to find this shoe store, they'd have to do it on their own.

Still. They couldn't disobey Pop.

The cable car rumbled to a brief stop. People hopped off, laden with shopping bags.

Andrew and Evie locked glances for a moment. "Are you coming or not?" Andrew asked.

"A promise is a promise," Evie said, shaking her head. "And big trouble is big trouble."

The bell rang again. Andrew paused, uncertain.

Then, as the car began to move down the hill, he turned and jumped onboard.

Chapter Four

"Wait!" Evie shouted.

Holding onto a pole, Andrew leaned out with his arm stretched. "Hurry!"

He grinned. Deep down inside, his nice, obedient sister was a pushover.

She was not, however, a track star. The driver waited for her at the next stop, and she climbed aboard, huffing and puffing. "Don't . . . ever . . . do that . . . again!" she sputtered, collapsing onto a seat.

As the car rolled on, Andrew felt the cool wind against his face. They passed shops with the oddest names — Juiced with Java, Wiki-Waki Wireless, Cutso's Cuts, Daze of Olde, Roger's in Heaven, Slops on the Slope. On a hill to his left, he could see the old cylindrical Coit Tower rising like an inland lighthouse above the tops of apartment buildings. To his right were the high, arched windows of the San Francisco Cable Car Museum. But no Van Ness Shoes.

Andrew made his way to the front of the car. There, a man with forearms like tree trunks pulled on the hinged grip of a long lever that rose from the floor. As he pulled and released, the car sped up and slowed down.

"Is that the brake?" Andrew asked.

"Nope," the man replied. "It's a cable grip. See those three tracks on the street? Two are for the wheels. The track in the middle is actually a long, narrow slot in the ground. The cable runs directly underneath, going round and round like an escalator, never stopping. This lever I'm operating? It goes right down through the car and into that slot. At the bottom of the lever is a grip. When I pull back, the grip tightens around the cable — and the cable pulls us along. Up to a maximum of nine and a half miles per hour."

"Cool," Andrew said. "Can I try?"

The man laughed. "Do you have a motorman's license?"

Evie came up from behind. "He's supposed to ask you where Van Ness Shoes is."

"That'd be Van Ness and Jackson, I believe," the man said. "You're a little far east. I'll let you off at the next stop and you can take the bus."

Van Ness was a long bus ride, but it was on the way

home. After getting off, Andrew and Evie raced toward Jackson Street. They almost missed the store. It was a small boutique with bare wood floors and soft techno pop playing over the speakers. The shoes were displayed on shelves in a busy arrangement at odd angles. Salespeople in black outfits walked around with little headphones and mouthpieces, like Secret Service agents.

It didn't take Andrew long to find the shoe that matched the orange-and-pink monstrosity Mom had sent them. It was on a sale rack against the back wall. Nineteen dollars and ninety-nine cents. And about three feet above their heads.

"What do we do now?" Andrew whispered.

"Is that the right shoe?" Evie asked.

"I think it's the left."

"I mean the *correct* shoe. Can you tell if it's your size?"

"Not from here. And even if it is, do we have enough money to buy it?"

Evie dug into her shoulder bag. "I have six dollars."

Andrew reached into his pocket, releasing a flood of candy wrappers and paper clips. "Three dollars and . . . seventy-two cents. If we buy only one shoe, do they give us half-price?"

A salesclerk, tall and thin with narrow glasses and a

pointed beard, slipped into the aisle. "May I help you?" he asked in a clipped, not-too-friendly voice.

"We need something in orange and pink," Evie replied.

"Just one," Andrew added.

"One pair?" the clerk said.

"No, one shoe," Andrew explained. "It's for my . . . cousin. He only wears one shoe. The left one. His right leg is much longer, which makes him walk lopsided. So if he goes barefoot — on the longer leg — it evens out."

Evie was maintaining her pleasant smile, but Andrew could feel her wishing the floor would open up and swallow him whole.

"I see," the clerk said. "Well, store policy permits only the sale of pairs, which I think you'll find is the case everywhere. But we do aim to satisfy our customers with special needs, so I suppose we could try to work out something with the store manager. Follow me, please."

Andrew eyed the bottom shelf of the display. If he stepped on it, he might be able to reach the shoe. That wouldn't be a bad idea. If there *was* a clue inside, he could quietly pocket it without the manager or the clerk seeing him. "You go," he said to Evie. "I want to stay and . . . browse."

The manager, a grim, dark-haired woman with sharp shoulders, was behind the cash register. As Evie and the clerk approached her, Andrew quickly took off his pack and let it fall to the floor.

He glanced over his shoulder. Evie, the clerk, and the manager had moved away from the desk. They were hidden from sight by a high, free-standing shoe rack.

Now.

Andrew stepped onto the bottom shelf. It gave a bit, groaning under his weight. He reached up as high as he could, his fingertips just grazing the sole of the sneaker.

Rats.

Andrew lowered himself. Then, bending his knees slightly, he jumped.

There. He had the heel between his thumb and forefinger. He held on tight as he came down, but the sneaker caught on the raised edge of the shelf. Andrew lost his balance. As his foot thumped down on the bottom shelf, it split with a sharp *crrracck*. He yelped, letting go of the sneaker and stumbling backward onto the floor.

The sneaker landed next to him. Something spilled out of it and hit the tiles with a loud smack. A cassette tape.

Andrew scooped it up and glanced at the label:

Out of the corner of his eye, he saw the manager and the clerk rushing toward him.

He shoved the tape into his pocket, tossed the shoe back onto the shelf, grabbed his pack, and ran.

"Excuse me!" the clerk shouted. "*Excuse me, young man!*"

Evie was still at the front of the store. Waving him on. "This way!" she shouted.

Together they pushed through the front door. "I have it!" Andrew shouted.

"The shoe?" Evie said, bursting out onto the sidewalk.

"The clue!" Andrew replied.

They ran right into two men dressed in black suits and sunglasses — one guy tall and spidery, the other thick and muscular.

"In a hurry?" the tall one said.

"We're not supposed to talk to strangers," Evie replied.

"I think they're the Men in Black," Andrew said lamely.

The stocky man smiled. "We work for the shoe store. Security. I'm Pudge, and this is Rafael."

"Why don't you show us what's in your backpack?" said Rafael.

Evie gave Andrew a for-once-in-your-life-don't-blow-it look, but he just smiled back at her. He was clean. He'd taken only the cassette — and who would ever accuse someone of stealing a cassette tape from a shoe store? He removed his pack and handed it to Rafael. "If you steal my Skittles, I'll press charges."

Evie elbowed him sharply.

Rafael unzipped the pack and pulled out the crate. "Hmm, what have we here?"

He lifted out an orange-and-pink sneaker — the one Andrew and Evie found in the crate.

Andrew blanched. "That one's ours!"

"Our . . . mother gave it to us," Evie said.

The guards gave each other a weary glance. "Would you step into the store, please?" Rafael asked.

Andrew tried to avoid Evie's poisonous look as they headed back inside Van Ness Shoes. Pudge pulled a cell phone from his belt and handed it to him. "On our way, you call home and tell your parents what happened."

Andrew's hand shook as he took the phone. Pop was going to kill him.

He tapped out his home number, praying for the answering machine. They were walking into the store now.

Staff, manager, and customers all stared at them as if they were serial killers.

"Hello, Wall residence," a familiar voice said.

"Hi, Pop," Andrew said feebly. "You'll never believe what happened today . . ."

Chapter Five

Evie held her stomach as the car sped over a steep hill. Pop was driving fast. He always drove fast when he was mad.

"We didn't try to steal anything," Andrew said for what must have been the twentieth time. "Honest."

"We'll discuss it when we're home." Pop's face was still, but his arms yanked the steering wheel a little too hard to the left.

Evie wanted to tell him to slow down, but she bit her lip. Pop was usually a reasonable guy but not today.

All in all, she and Andrew had been lucky back in Van Ness Shoes. They'd gotten away with little more than a sharp scolding and a vague threat about a police report. Pop did not find out about the crate. And Andrew had found something that might be extremely important — an old cassette in the left shoe. It had *clue* written all over it.

Did it mean that Mom had been in the store? That Mom was actually in San Francisco, at this minute —

lurking in school hallways and local shoe stores? Would they run into her on the street?

Evie imagined the look on Mom's face when they met for the first time in almost a year. Evie was at least two inches taller, Andrew three. Mom would be so proud. She'd insist on taking them shopping. She would say they were too thin and treat them to a feast. She would hold an 11 11 11 celebration, even though it was close to 11 11 12.

Evie hadn't wanted to tell Andrew — hadn't dared admit it — but when they moved here, she'd believed they'd lost Mom, too. It was easy to pretend to be optimistic in front of her brother. You could hide behind optimism. Real hope, somehow, was harder. It required opening yourself up — and that was the biggest risk. Because when things didn't work out, being open meant getting hurt.

Through the window she saw fantastic storefronts with odd names and, at an intersection, a sloping vista to the bay. But Andrew was slumped against the opposite car door, his hand firmly on the pocket that contained the cassette.

Soon Pop was turning into the driveway of their narrow, four-story house. "I want to talk to you briefly," he said, "inside."

They piled out of the car and through the side door into the basement. Andrew and Evie sat on an old yellow sofa left over from the last tenants, and Pop pulled up a chair across from the coffee table, which was empty except for a WELCOME TO THE NEIGHBORHOOD brochure left by the real-estate agent.

"People make stupid mistakes in life," Pop said softly. "Goodness knows I've made my own. But this — this was a big one."

"But it — we didn't —" Andrew stammered.

"We broke your rule, Pop, and we're sorry," Evie interrupted. "We will never do it again."

"My rule is the least of it," Pop said. "Shoplifting is a serious crime —"

"But we didn't —" Andrew began.

Evie squelched her brother's sentence with a poisonous glance, stifling any attempt at explaining why they *happened* to have one orange-and-pink sneaker that matched the one in the store.

"This shouldn't come as a surprise," Pop said, "but I'm grounding you. Totally. I didn't think I'd have to do this — but I didn't think you'd ever abuse my trust like this. I'm having a tough enough time getting used to CHQ here in San Francisco. I don't need to worry about you two running off and getting into trouble. Now, go upstairs to your rooms. If you don't have much homework, finish unpacking."

Evie and Andrew both nodded solemnly. Adjusting to CHQ — Company Headquarters — was always a big thing for Pop. He hated it. It always made him grouchy.

They marched up three flights to their floor. "Mom sent us a cassette player," Evie whispered. "Let's go to my room and play that tape."

Andrew dropped his backpack on Evie's bed and fished the tape out of his pocket. He showed Evie the label.

"E. Caparac?" she said. "Do you recognize that name?"

"Nope." From his pack, Andrew pulled the cassette player Mom had included in the crate. He flipped open the top, and popped in the tape. As he pressed PLAY, the tape player's mechanism whirred and whined. "Rrraaacchh . . . wwooor . . . zzzhaaaan . . . eeb . . ." a voice caterwauled, to a background of music that sounded like an underwater torture chamber.

"Mom is into some weird stuff," Andrew said, lowering the volume.

"Mom's machine is *broken*," Evie groaned. "It's playing backward!"

"Maybe it's the tape, not the machine," Andrew said. "Let's test it with another tape. I packed a bunch we used to listen to in the car."

He ran into his room and returned with a tape. Evie glanced at the label. " 'Tubby the Tuba'?"

"It was my favorite," Andrew said, popping the tape into the recorder.

"Mrrrroooaaaawwwwp . . ." the tape groaned.

"Tubby hasn't aged well," Evie said.

Andrew snapped off the player. "You were right. The machine is busted. We need another one. I saw an electronics store on the way home. We could tell Pop we need it for a school project — an oral history report or something. If he won't let us get it, maybe he can pick one up himself."

"Just don't get us in trouble again. Pop won't ground us next time, he'll hire the FBI."

They rushed downstairs. But as they reached the second-floor landing, the doorbell rang.

Evie stopped, holding her brother back. "Uh-oh. Andrew, did that guy at the store file a police report?"

"I don't know," Andrew said, eyeing the door. "If we go to jail, will it go on our permanent records?"

They huddled at the top of the stairs, looking down

as Pop walked into the foyer from the living room. His back was to them as he pulled open the front door.

A smiling young woman stood at the door, clutching a small shoulder bag. Her hair was a vibrant brown, falling past her shoulders in silken waves that seemed almost liquid. As she stepped into the foyer, her eyes picked up the light from the chandelier.

She was the most beautiful woman Evie had ever seen.

"Marisol," Pop said, smiling.

"Hello, Richard," the young woman answered.

"Not a cop," Andrew whispered.

Pop took the woman's coat and hung it on the rack. "You have no idea what a relief it was to find you."

Marisol giggled. "Do the kids know?"

Andrew and Evie instinctively shrank back, out of sight.

"No, not yet," Pop said. "I didn't dare tell them in advance. I wanted them to meet you first."

Evie clenched up. In her darkest moments she'd imagined all kinds of awful things happening. But Pop finding a *girlfriend*? The notion had never even crossed her mind. Her hopes — for Mom's return, for their family to be together again — were slowly dying.

Her brother looked as if his blood had turned to milk.

Marisol and Pop were in the kitchen now. Their voices were muffled and soft behind the thick walls and floors of the old house. But her laugh, soft and musical, was like fingernails on glass.

"I can't stand this," Andrew said, tiptoeing back upstairs.

He ran into Evie's room and grabbed the iPod.

"Are you crazy?" Evie whispered, tiptoeing into the room behind him. "We can't eavesdrop on them! It's one thing to spy on strangers — but we can't spy on Pop."

Evie held out her hand. Reluctantly, Andrew gave her the iPod.

"It's not fair for him to do this to us and keep it a secret," he protested. "Did he know her in Connecticut, too? Can't he wait for Mom? Is he that impatient? *It's not fair*!" Andrew picked up the cassette from the shoe store, slammed it into the machine, pressed PLAY, and cranked up the volume.

"*R R R A A A C C H H . . . W W O O O R . . . ZZZHAAAAN . . . EEB . . .*"

"Andrew, what are you doing?" Evie said.

"I'm going to make this house unbearable," Andrew said, banging out a loud beat on the wall, "so she'll *never* want to come back."

Evie reached for the OFF button. But her hand paused just above the machine.

The tape was saying something. Real words, from the sound of it — only Andrew was pounding so loudly, she couldn't understand them. "Stop it!" she shouted. "*Listen!*"

Andrew's arms dropped to his sides.

Evie lowered the volume, rewound the tape a bit, and pressed PLAY.

The tape whirred to life.

"*Zhhhhaam . . . orloob . . . mo-o-other's innnn he-e-eaven . . . MO-O-OTHER'S INNNN HE-E-EAVEN . . .*"

Chapter Six

"Vote for Doreen!"

"Yu for You!"

As Andrew walked onto the playground the next morning, he ignored the candidates just inside the gate. He wasn't hearing their chants. As far as he was concerned, Doreen could keep the stupid onyx stone he'd given her. It didn't matter anymore. Nothing mattered.

Mother's in heaven.

Andrew could not get the words out of his mind. All night long he heard the garbled phrase in his imagination. It kept him from sleeping. Haunted him.

And now, the next morning, on the school playground, he couldn't think straight. Last night seemed like a cruel nightmare. Pop had a *girlfriend*. Pop, who had crabbed at them all morning, who had insisted on driving them to school — and then stood and watched sternly as they walked through the gates. Like they were first graders.

Over the entire *year* — ever since Mom had vanished — Pop had been acting strange. He'd hardly talked about her. As if, all along, he knew she wasn't coming back.

Mother's in heaven.

Mom hadn't sent the crate — not with a message like that. Obviously. So who *had* sent it? Mom had enemies, that much he knew. But would anyone stoop to something like this? Planting the crate and the cassette — just to shock Andrew and Evie?

He looked at his sister. Today, she was the one in her own world. In one hand she held the WELCOME TO YOUR NEIGHBORHOOD brochure they'd gotten in the mail, which she was reading intently. In the other hand was the cassette recorder, which Evie was listening to with a set of earphones. The weird thing was, she was playing that creepy message over and over.

"Evie, how can you listen to that?" he said.

"It's not 'mother' . . ." she replied.

"Of course it's not! How could she have sent —?"

"That's not what I mean — just listen." Evie pulled off the earphones, wrapped them around his head, and played the tape.

Andrew heard the familiar static fill his ears — the words welling up, so *loud* —

He reached up to pull them off, then stopped.

50

This close, the whole thing sounded different. The words seemed less human, more mechanical and unclear. Like actual backward speech, not planted words. Speech that only *sort of* sounded like words.

"It's like . . . Modger's in heaven," Andrew remarked.

Evie was beaming. "Andrew, on the cable car ride we passed a lot of funky old shops with weird names. Remember?"

She held out the brochure. It was an illustrated view of the blocks around their neighborhood. On the left side was the street where they had climbed in the cable car. As Evie ran her finger up the map, Andrew recognized some of the shop names he'd seen: Juiced with Java . . . Wiki-Waki Wireless . . . Cutso's Cuts . . .

Her finger stopped when it reached a shop near Coit Tower.

" 'Roger's in Heaven' . . ." Andrew read aloud.

"Yes — *Roger's*! Not *Mother's*. Not *Modgers*," Evie said. "It's the place where Mom wants us to go next. To pick up the next clue."

Andrew pressed REVERSE and played the tape again. And again. "So Mom isn't . . . ?"

Evie smiled. "You know Mom. Always one step ahead."

"*Woo-hah*!" Andrew shouted. Grinning, he looked over his shoulder. Pop was gone. The sun was bright, the air cool, and Mom was *alive*.

ALIVE! He started jumping up and down. He felt about three years old. He pulled out the cassette tape and began kissing it. "E. Caparac," he announced, reading the tape's label, "we love you."

"You are so embarrassing," Evie said, hiding her face.

Andrew stared at the label — that name . . . E. CAPARAC. "Is that Mom's handwriting?"

Evie looked over his shoulder. "I can't tell. It could be, if she were in a hurry."

"Sounds weird. If Mom wrote it, it probably means something. Sounds Greek maybe. Like E Pluribus Unum."

"That's Latin. Besides, Mom doesn't do languages, she does codes."

"And backward recording mechanisms . . ."

That was it — *backward. If the tape were recorded backward,* Andrew thought, *could the label have been written that way, too?*

He sounded the word backward: "Ca . . . ra . . . pace. Carapace. Hey, is that a word?"

"That's what a turtle has on its back. A shell. A covering!" Evie said. "Andrew, that's great! Mom wants us to find the cassette's *shell* — its plastic box. At Roger's in Heaven. There's probably a message on it."

Andrew pocketed the tape. "We'll go during lunch. We can hop on a bus or a cable car, visit the place, and be back before the next period. Forty minutes, tops."

"We can't!"

"Why?"

"First of all, Mr. Xing told us it's against school rules to travel that far away during lunch, unless it's to go home. Second, we *won't* make it back in time. And third, we're *grounded!*"

"Well, now that we've discussed the pros and cons," Andrew said with a shrug, "what do you think?"

Evie dumped the cassette player in her backpack and headed for the door. "Meet me here after the lunch bell. If you're a minute late, the trip is off."

As the rest of Adolph Green Middle School settled into their sandwiches, Andrew and Evie jumped off the cable car on a street that sloped down to Fisherman's Wharf. They sprinted up a quiet side street toward the ROGER'S IN HEAVEN logo painted in faded psychedelic balloon letters outside a small storefront. On the way in, Andrew glanced at the window, chock full of old vinyl albums with names like Moby Grape, Three Dog Night, and Creedence Clearwater Revival.

He pushed open the door and stepped onto a creaky linoleum floor worn to bare wood beneath. The chords of a classic rock song echoed into the high ceilings. Early Stones, maybe. Posters overwhelmed the walls, saggy and billowing from neglect: Jimi Hendrix, all sinew and cheekbone and fingers under a mountain of hair. Janis Joplin, screaming into a mike as if her life depended on it. Tina Turner, young and thin . . .

"Forty minutes, you said forty minutes," Evie hissed. "It already took us nineteen to get here."

"Right." Andrew fished the cassette out of his pocket and approached a man who sat on a stool behind a pitted, solid-wood counter. He wore a weather-beaten leather hat pressed over an unruly thatch of silver-white hair, and the wire-rim glasses perched near the end of his nose gave him the look of an aging, slightly overweight elf. His name tag — CLAUDE — was nearly lost in a vest festooned with buttons, including one that said MCCARTHY FOR PRESIDENT '68 and another that said SPEAK LOUDER, I BLEW OUT MY EARS AT WOODSTOCK.

"*Hello, Mr. Claude, sir! I have a question!*" Evie shouted.

Claude looked up with a start. "Lord, I have to stop wearing that button," he murmured. "What can I do for you?"

Andrew tentatively held out the cassette. "We need the cover for this, for . . . er, a history report. But we don't know the name of the group."

The man peered at it through his glasses, then turned to the wall behind him. As he lifted the arm of a spinning turntable, the rock song abruptly stopped, and he popped the cassette into a player.

A song rang out — folksy and corny, full of acoustical guitars and cheery voices singing about fields of woe and waves of peace, or maybe it was waves of woe and fields of peace. Andrew wasn't so sure he liked the tape played forward any better than he liked it backward.

"Ha!" Claude laughed. "You little prankster, you know *exactly* who they are, don't you?"

Andrew gave his sister a look. "We do?"

"The Sugar Shop, of course!" Claude said. "I named my store after one of their songs. They were hot for awhile in the sixties. Pretty mediocre, actually — watered-down Mamas and Papas — but all the girls went nuts over their drummer, Roger Gilpin. Well, one day it gets out that if you play the first track backward, you can hear a secret message . . ."

"Roger's in Heaven?" Evie said.

Claude grinned. "Between you and me, I thought it sounded more like Mutchers in Heaven —"

"Or Modgers," Andrew added.

"Anyway, the fans went crazy, sales went sky high, even though old Roger was alive, strong as a bull, and laughing all the way to the bank. I always thought it'd be a funny name for a store — and you're the only people without arthritis and wrinkles ever to get the joke!"

"Do you have any of their cassettes?" Andrew asked.

"You can check, but I doubt it," Claude replied with a sigh, giving Andrew back his tape. "Methinks you've got a collector's item here, fella. I haven't seen one of those tapes in at least ten years."

Evie tapped her watch. "Eleven minutes," she whispered.

Andrew thanked Claude and he and Evie hurried to the cassette section, which was against a back wall. Andrew eyed the plastic dividers, stopping at S, and began riffling through.

And there it was. Wedged between *Sufi Dervish Chants* and *The Supremes*.

Andrew pulled out a dusty cassette box with a washed-out label. The words SUGAR SHOP spilled across a blue-skied meadow in which four hippies sang with flow-

ers in their ears, instruments in hand, and some power-
fully ugly clothes. One man, playing the upright bass,
bore a strong resemblance to Claude.

"Okay, now what?" Evie asked.

Andrew flipped open the box. It was empty — except
for a small folded sheet. Liner notes, he figured.

He opened the sheet and glanced at the list of songs:

```
Sailor's greeting
Where a lion lives
To mark up text with
   corrections
Boiling mad
___ the Red
Noon in PST is 3:00 P.M. here
First lady
Where a bee lives
Paid no attention to
Took in a breath
Barbie's boyfriend
An astrological sign
"___ go, Mets!"
Title of graphic novel by Art
   Spiegelman
Head motion that means yes
```

```
Not "evens"
Exclamations of surprise
Like yesterday's pizza or dinosaur
    bones
Shout at a bullfight
Busting your buttons
Simon ___
Farm tower
Nine on a diamond
Do re mi fa sol la __ do
Your waiter appreciates this
```

"Evie . . . ?" Andrew said.

But his sister was already out on the street. "*Andrew, come on, the bus is here!*" she cried out.

Andrew grabbed the paper and the cassette box, shoved them into his pocket, and ran. "*Methinks we have another clue!*"

The bus took off just as he reached the sidewalk.

Evie looked up and down the hill. Nothing was coming — cable car or bus. "Methinks we're toast."

Chapter Seven

"I know, it's hard to adjust to the rules of a new school," said Ms. Skinner, the principal of Adolph Green Middle School, "but in order to create an open and free environment, we must have strict limits. So let's call this an *adjustment*, not detention."

Andrew nodded obediently. Ms. Skinner seemed young and friendly, and her office was comfortable enough, with a round, blond wood table, padded seats, and a bookcase that divided the table from the principal's desk. But as far as Andrew was concerned, detention was detention. And Big Trouble was Big Trouble.

"You're not going to tell our father, are you, Ms. Skinner?" he asked.

"We've learned our lesson," Evie added. "Totally."

Ms. Skinner laughed. "Well, it's not as if you perpetrated any great harm to society. I trust you won't do this again. So I'll agree not to call your dad if you agree to give me a thoughtful three-page essay on nutrition and the value of a good lunch. You can use the *Encyclopedia Britannica* on my shelf."

As she walked away, Andrew muttered, "Three pages?"

Evie was already taking the N volume from the shelf. She leafed through until she found NUTRITION. "You do food groups. I'll do vitamins, protein, carbohydrates, fat. We'll be out of here in no time."

She began writing furiously, which immediately gave Andrew a headache. He removed his notebook from his backpack slowly. The sheet he'd found at Roger's in Heaven was wedged between the pages. He was dying to look at it again, but first things first.

The food groups are arranged in a pyramid, he wrote, *with the stuff you're supposed to eat less of at the top, like fats and sweets and all the things a kid really likes.*

It was terrible. But he wasn't expecting to be graded, so he kept going. With the description and a generous drawing of the pyramid itself, he filled a page and a half easily.

Evie was still absorbed in her masterpiece, so Andrew quietly flattened out the clue sheet and looked at the first line:

Sailor's greeting

Yo ho ho?

Where a lion lives

Savanna? Den? Zoo?

Why were these clues so vague? Mom was too good to leave vague clues.

Unless it wasn't Mom who was leaving them. Or unless Andrew was missing something. Some other key to solving the puzzle.

He looked at the scrawl down the right-hand side of the sheet.

If you turned them on their side, they looked like words. Sort of.

ENTER IN GRID

HIDDEN IN PLAIN SIGHT

Evie snapped open her loose-leaf notebook and removed four pages. "Done! I included the regular food pyramid, its original and updated versions, and also the vegetarian food pyramid."

"*I* did that," Andrew said. "Well, some of it . . ."

Evie looked at Andrew's sheet. "Gadzooks! Hallelu-jah! Woo-hoo! Wheeeee!"

"No need to be sarcastic."

"Sorry, I was answering that clue — 'exclamations of surprise.' It could mean a million different things," Evie said. "Why are you holding it sideways?"

"Because of this scrawl. I'm thinking it might be the code key."

"Well, they look like words. *Half* words. Like mirror writing." Evie took out scissors from her pack and carefully cut the words into six strips:

A TO Z ANSWERS
ENTER IN GRID
DOWN & TO RT ONLY
LINES SEPARATE WORKS
HIDDEN IN PLAIN SIGHT
TOP L TO BOTTOM R

"Nah, not mirror writing," Andrew said, flipping two of the strips over:

A TO Z ANSWERS
ENTER IN GRID
DOWN & TO RT ONLY
LINES SEPARATE WORDS

"You're right, they're just plain old half words!" With her pen, Evie began filling in the missing halves:

A TO Z ANSWERS
ENTER IN GRID
DOWN & TO RT ONLY
LINES SEPARATE WORDS
HIDDEN IN PLAIN SIGHT
TOP L TO BOTTOM R

" 'A to Z answers,' " Andrew read. "That must mean the answers will be in alphabetical order from A to Z —"

" 'Enter in grid'?" Evie said. "What grid?"

"Mom sent us graph paper in the crate," Andrew said. "We'll have to look at it."

Evie nodded. "And then we'll enter the words 'down and to the right only.' But I don't get the last instructions — 'lines separate words,' 'hidden in plain sight,' and 'top l to bottom r.' "

"We'll have to figure that out later." Andrew looked at the sheet of clues. "Okay, here we go. A to Z. First clue — 'sailor's greeting' —"

"AHOY!" Evie blurted out.

"Good." Andrew filled it in. "So the second one . . . 'where a lion lives'? Den? Savanna?"

"Den. Because the *third* clue is 'to mark up text for corrections' — which would be edit," Evie said.

Andrew wrote in the first three answers.

```
Sailor's greeting            AHOY
Where a lion lives            DEN
To mark up text with corrections  EDIT
```

"Next clue — what's 'boiling mad'?" Evie asked.

Andrew thought for a moment. "Hang on. Let me think . . ."

The door opened and Doreen entered, holding a clipboard. "Oh, deeear," she said, "detention. When I'm president, I'll make sure that students can stand up for their rights against —"

"Hello, Doreen," Ms. Skinner said, walking over from her side of the office.

Doreen smiled brightly. "Here are the attendance sheets I've collected from all the eighth-grade teachers. I can do seventh if that will be helpful."

"No, thank you, Doreen."

With a cheery wave, Doreen left.

"Speaking of boiling mad . . ." Evie said.

"What was that?" Ms. Skinner asked sharply.

Evie quickly hid the clue sheet under her loose-leaf notebook. "My brother is still boiling mad at himself for misbehaving. But he's happy to say our report is done."

Andrew smiled. "Well . . . not boiling mad, really. What's the word for it . . . ?"

"A little angry?" Evie chimed in. "Slightly furious?"

Ms. Skinner smiled. "Mildly perturbed? A bit enraged?"

"Enraged!" Andrew nearly shouted. "Yes! Enraged works! Thank you so much! Thank you!"

He and Evie were out the door before Ms. Skinner could reply.

A few blocks from the school, they'd managed to nail most of the clues. But not all.

" 'The First Lady'?" Evie mentally inserted the name of the President's wife into the list of answers. "*Her* name doesn't fit alphabetically."

"And who is Art Spiegelman?" Andrew asked.

They both examined the list carefully:

Sailor's greeting	AHOY
Where a lion lives	DEN
To mark up text with corrections	EDIT
Boiling mad	ENRAGED
___ the Red	ERIK or ERIC

Noon in PST is
   3:00 P.M. here   EST
First lady
Where a bee lives   HIVE
Paid no attention to   IGNORED
Took in a breath   INHALED
Barbie's boyfriend   KEN
An astrological sign
"___ go, Mets!"   LET'S
Title of graphic
   novel by Art Spiegelman
Head motion that means yes NOD
Not "evens"   ODDS
Exclamations of surprise   OHS
Like yesterday's pizza
   or dinosaur bones   OLD
Shout at a bullfight   OLE
Busting your buttons   PROUD
Simon ___
Farm tower
Nine on a diamond
Do re mi fa sol la __ do   TI
Your waiter appreciates this

"Whatever we can't guess," Andrew said, "we can Google."

As they turned the corner to their house, Evie put away the sheet. Pop's car was in the driveway, and a white Volkswagen Beetle with pink trim and California plates was parked in front.

"I thought he was at work," Evie said.

"Maybe he's meeting the boss here," Andrew said.

"The boss drives a pink-and-white Beetle?"

They climbed the stoop and pushed open the front door. "Pop?" Andrew called out.

"In here!" Pop replied from the living room.

The twins followed his voice. They found Pop standing in the living room's wide, arched entryway. Their area rugs and furniture were in place, arranged in front of the cozy fireplace. A couple of padded armchairs and two black-leather sofas faced each other across a glass coffee table. On one of the sofas was the person Andrew and Evie least wanted to see.

"Hi, I'm Marisol," she said, standing up, looking even more beautiful than when they'd seen her from the top of the stairs.

Pop smiled uncomfortably at Andrew and Evie. "I hope you'll be nice, because you'll be seeing a lot of Marisol around here."

"We will?" Andrew squeaked. His stomach felt like a fist.

"Your father and I have gotten to know each other well recently," Marisol said. "He's a great guy, so I'm sure you two are just as wonderful."

"It's very important that you two . . . feel *comfortable* with a new woman around the house," Pop said.

Andrew sank quietly into the opposite sofa. Marisol was radiant. She seemed sweet, too.

He hated her.

Evie was still standing, her hands clutching the top of an armchair. Her mouth quivered. "So . . . so you've decided," she said.

"I'm afraid so," Pop said solemnly.

Evie sighed. "When's the big date?"

Marisol's jaw dropped. "Date?"

"You know . . . the *wedding*," Andrew said.

"Oh, my goodness no," Pop said, fighting back a smile. "I've *hired* Marisol. She's a college student. She'll pick you up from school every day and help you with homework until I come home."

"She will?" Andrew said. "Why?"

"Marisol," Pop said patiently, "is your new nanny."

Chapter Eight

"Who does he think he is?" Evie thundered. She pulled up her shade, letting the morning sun into her bedroom. "Who does she think *she* is — Mary Poppins? Like we're *babies*?"

"Pop told her I have trouble with math," Andrew said, setting the crate on his sister's bedroom carpet. "I *don't* have trouble with math — well, not too much."

"At least she's not our new mom," Evie said.

Andrew didn't want to think about it. He took out the graph paper and unfolded it. In the middle, drawn in marker, was a strange crossword grid. "I found our grid," he said, looking at it carefully.

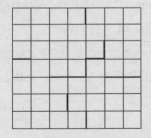

Evie stared at the Google page loading on her monitor. "*Maus*," she murmured.

"Huh?" Andrew replied.

"The book by Art Spiegelman — it's a graphic novel about a little mouse caught up in the Holocaust." As Evie surfed the Web trying to find answers to clues, she smelled bacon and eggs wafting all the way up from the first floor. Pop was being especially nice to them after the bombshell he'd dropped last night.

"Anyway, having a sitter is almost worse than having a new mom," Andrew said, carefully unfolding the clue sheet and penciling in MAUS. "We'll never be alone. How can we follow Mom's scavenger hunt if *we're* being followed?"

The White House Web site appeared on the screen. "Hmm, nothing on the First Lady," Evie said. "She doesn't fit alphabetically with the other answers — first or last name, maiden name, nothing."

"There must be some kind of trick to it. First lady . . . could it be, like, Priscilla Alden? Wasn't she the first lady in America from the Mayflower?"

"That is *so* Eurocentric," Evie said.

"Evie? Andrew?" Pop's voice called upstairs. "Time for breakfast!"

"Okay, Pop!" Andrew called back.

"What about the first lady of all time?" Evie said. "Like, those bones they found in Africa. That prehistoric, apelike woman. They called her something . . . what was the name? Lucy?"

"Eve!" Andrew said.

Evie sneered. "So funny I forgot to laugh . . ."

"No — Eve! *Adam's* Eve. The first lady ever! That works!"

Yes. Puns. Word play. That was so Mom.

Andrew quickly scanned the missing answers:

```
Busting your buttons        PROUD
Simon ___
Farm tower
Nine on a diamond
Do re mi fa sol la __ do     TI
Your waiter appreciates
   this
```

"We can nail this," Andrew said. "What kind of tower is on a farm? — and it has to begin with a P, S, or T. Think of word play. Tower could be, like, a tow truck . . . *tow*-er?"

Evie rolled her eyes. "Duh, how about a *silo*?" she said, scribbling in the answer. "Okay, 'nine on a diamond' . . ."

Carats? Andrew thought. No, that starts with a C. *Facets* — diamonds have facets. But that's F. OK, then, what other kinds of diamonds were there? He thought of one of Pop's old cassettes: *Neil Diamond . . . Diamond salt . . . baseball diamond . . .*

"Bingo. Nine people on a baseball team," Evie said, writing TEAM after the clue.

"Tip!" Andrew blurted out triumphantly. "That's what waiters appreciate!"

"One more," Evie said.

From below, Pop's voice boomed up, a little louder and more tense: *"Simon says . . . come down and eat!"*

Andrew glanced at his sister and grinned.

SAYS, he wrote on the sheet's only remaining blank spot, and they both raced downstairs for breakfast.

"VOTE DOREEN FOR ADOLPH GREEN!"

"SARAH YU FOR ME AND YOU!"

Evie and Andrew were nearly mowed down by the throng of students gathered inside the cafeteria at lunch period. The candidates had set up tables right near the entrance. Sarah was handing out Student Council refrigerator magnets. Doreen had a huge box of chocolate bars. Her friends were passing them around the cafeteria.

Grabbing a Snickers, Andrew joined Evie in line to vote. A faculty adviser, Mr. Sweeney, was collecting ballots at a lunch table. "Girls, no electioneering, please!" he shouted wearily.

"Does Doreen have the onyx?" Evie asked.

"How should I know?" Andrew said. "I can't ask her. She's too busy shouting."

Following the instructions taped to the table, they wrote their choices — both wrote SARAH YU — on their ballots, sealed the ballots in envelopes, and signed the outside of their envelopes. Then they headed to the back of the room.

"I fuh guffee," Andrew mumbled.

"Once more, with mouth empty," Evie said, sitting at a secluded table.

Andrew swallowed. "I feel guilty, eating Doreen's chocolate and voting for Sarah."

"Especially after she called you cute. Well, you'll have to work that out later." Evie laid out the clue sheet, the grid, and the decoded key:

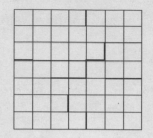

A TO Z ANSWERS
ENTER IN GRID
DOWN & TO RT ONLY
LINES SEPARATE WORDS
HIDDEN IN PLAIN SIGHT
TOP L TO BOTTOM R

Sailor's greeting	AHOY
Where a lion lives	DEN
To mark up text with corrections	EDIT
Boiling mad	ENRAGED
___ the Red	ERIK OR ERIC
Noon in PST is 3:00 P.M. here	EST
First lady	EVE
Where a bee lives	HIVE
Paid no attention to	IGNORED
Took in a breath	INHALED
Barbie's boyfriend	KEN
An astrological sign	LEO
"___ go, Mets!"	LETS
Title of graphic novel by Art Spiegelman	MAUS

Head motion that means yes	NOD
Not "evens"	ODDS
Exclamations of surprise	OHS
Like yesterday's pizza or dinosaur bones	OLD
Shout at a bullfight	OLE
Busting your buttons	PROUD
Simon ___	SAYS
Farm tower	SILO
Nine on a diamond	TEAM
Do re mi fa sol la ___ do	TI
Your waiter appreicates this	TIP

"We enter these words into the grid, down and to the right," she said. "But how? Crossword puzzles are supposed to have numbers — like 1 Down, 2 Across. Also blank boxes in between words. This is just a regular old grid."

"Except for the little dark lines," Andrew said. "Some are vertical and some are horizontal. They're the things that *separate the words* — just like in the instruction. So we fit the words between them."

"Excellent!" Evie said. "Let's start with the smallest word, *ti*. There's only one place it'll fit."

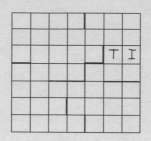

Andrew nodded. "Okay. The four-letter word that goes down through the *I* — that could be ERIC or EDIT."

"But the one next to it, which goes through the T . . ." Evie scanned the list of clues. "That can only be LETS."

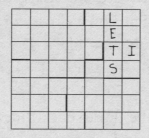

Andrew pointed to the three boxes going across the L. "OLE is the only one that fits here."

"And the only one that can use the S of LETS is EST!" Evie said.

				O	L	E
					E	
					T	I
				E	S	T

"That decides EDIT and ERIK," Andrew said, writing fast. "And the E of EST starts ERIK . . . with a K — because good old KEN fits at the bottom."

				O	L	E
					E	D
					T	I
				E	S	T
				R		
				I		
				K	E	N

"Where he belongs," Evie added. "So now I see a place for HIVE and DEN and EVE —"

"And OHS and IGNORED . . ."

They worked through the election, through lunch, and didn't look up until finally the whole grid was filled:

T	E	A	M	O	L	E
I	N	H	A	L	E	D
P	R	O	U	D	T	I
S	A	Y	S	E	S	T
I	G	N	O	R	E	D
L	E	O	H	I	V	E
O	D	D	S	K	E	N

"We are *geniuses*!" Evie shouted.

Andrew scratched his head. "Maybe. But how does this help us find Mom?"

Thhhwock!

From the other corner of the cafeteria, a chair thumped to the floor. "FOOD FIGHT!" someone yelled.

Mr. Sweeney leaped up to intervene as everyone ran to see what was happening.

Three of Doreen's friends were throwing wads of stuff that looked like spinach. Andrew recognized the guys right away. They were the ones who'd given him the Snickers bar.

Evie folded up the crossword sheet. "Come on!" she said.

As Andrew followed her across the room, he kept his eye on the ballot table. Doreen was lingering near it, fiddling with her hair.

Andrew stayed on the edge of the crowd, watching her closely despite the frenzy of the fight around them. He reached into his backpack for the binoculars, lifted them to his eyes, and ducked behind a table to watch her inconspicuously.

Looking left and right, Doreen edged closer to the ballot box. She snatched it up, sank behind the table, and began pulling ballots out by the fistful, frantically reading each one.

Andrew felt a circular depression in the binoculars, right where his right index finger was. And he realized exactly how smart Mom was. In Connecticut he had lost his telescope, which doubled secretly as a digital camera. Mom had sent these binoculars as a replacement.

He aimed the binoculars and pressed his index finger firmly. A small LCD screen popped out the top of the binoculars, showing the image of Doreen ravaging the ballot box. With a barely audible click, Andrew took a photo.

Chapter Nine

"She's *what*?" Evie turned from the food fight, where three boys now lay on the floor, covered with green glop. They were laughing hysterically.

"Rigging the election — just like she said!" Andrew said.

He raced through the crowd with Evie close behind, heading for the ballot table. But Doreen was fast. She was walking away now, looking chipper and innocent. The box lay on the table as if nothing had ever happened.

"Doreen, you are sneaky and unethical," Evie said, "and if you think you can stuff that ballot box without anyone seeing it, you are so wrong!"

Doreen folded her arms defiantly. "Oh? You're accusing me of election fraud? Now *why* would a front runner stoop to something like that? Where are your witnesses?"

"The photographic eye never lies!" Andrew said, turning the binoculars' LCD window to Doreen and scrolling to the last image. "Behold!"

On the small screen, a blur of jeans and shirttail materialized.

Doreen burst out laughing. "Sammy Snider's behind?"

Andrew dropped the binoculars back into his pack. "Well, I saw you!"

"You did?" Doreen held out her arms. "Check my pockets. Check my pack. Check the box. If you're going to try to ruin my reputation, you'd better have some evidence — because if you don't, I will bring you up on charges of defamation of character, and you can kiss your careers at Adolph Green good-bye."

"I hate her," Evie said as she and Andrew walked toward the lobby after school. "She's rotten and creepy. She took Mom's stone."

"She spoiled my lunch period," Andrew grumbled.

As they passed the principal's office, Andrew glanced inside. The ballot box was in there somewhere. It would sit there over the weekend until Monday morning, when the ballots would be counted.

"We have two days," Andrew said. "We can nail her, Evie. She must have the ballots. It's up to us to find them. I can follow her home, sneak a photo. I can use the iPod mike to record her. We'll get *something*."

"We have to find Mom," Evie said with a sigh. "Forget Doreen."

"Just give me an hour." Andrew stopped just before they reached the lobby and peered around the corner. Through the school's glass front doors she could see Marisol waiting by the curb, leaning against her car. "Look, you tell Marisol I had to stay after for help in math — she'll believe that. Tell her she'll have to pick me up in an hour. I'll be back by then."

Evie thought about it for a moment. "Okay. One hour. And if you don't find anything, you give it up. Deal?"

"Deal."

Andrew stood against the wall as Evie left. He counted to one hundred, slowly, then peeked out again.

Marisol's car was gone.

And Doreen was heading toward the door. As usual, she was surrounded by friends, including Rosie.

Andrew shrank back again and waited. He took his iPod from his pack and put it in one pocket, then stashed the binoculars in the other. Doreen's conversation was about eighty percent brand names and twenty percent real words, and it seemed to go on for hours. But when she finally left, he made his move.

Doreen and Rosie were peeling away from the others, heading west.

Andrew scampered after them, keeping a half-block distance. The sidewalks were full, and the storefronts made perfect hiding places.

He slipped behind fruit stands. He picked up newspapers and covered his face. Tailing people in San Francisco was easy. Doreen and Rosie didn't suspect a thing.

They turned up a sunny, tree-lined street with attached houses all painted bright pastel colors. From behind a mailbox, Andrew watched the girls turn into a light-blue house with a small lawn surrounded by bushes.

Keeping behind cars that were parked along the curb, Andrew sneaked close to the house. He switched on his iPod and inserted the earphones.

The girls were laughing. "They are so stupid," Rosie's voice came through the mike. "Ugly, too."

Easy, pal, Andrew said to himself. Stupid was a matter of opinion, but *ugly*? They couldn't have been talking about Evie and him.

They disappeared inside the house, and the voices stopped. In a moment he saw the two girls through the front bay window, flopping onto the sofa.

Their voices might be audible through the glass. But he'd have to get closer to know for sure.

Andrew came out from behind the cars. Keeping low, he scurried onto the sidewalk and behind a bush.

The voices were louder but muffled. Through the leaves he could see Doreen reaching into her pack and pulling out . . . what?

He put his binoculars to his eyes and adjusted the zoom, pulling her image closer to him . . .

VRROOOOOOM!

An explosion of engine noise pounded his ears. Stifling a scream, Andrew yanked out the ear phones.

He looked over his shoulder. Two enormous motorcycles, chrome-covered and glaring in the reflecting sunlight, roared past him. Riding one was a mountainous man with a flowing gray beard, a scar running down his right cheek, and a network of tattoos on his biceps. On the other was a ruddy-faced woman with square shoulders and intense green eyes.

The engines chuffed and slowed. Then both bikes turned into Doreen's driveway.

Andrew curled up tighter behind the bush. The engine noise stopped. He heard the creak of kickstands moving into place.

What were they *doing* here?

Maybe Doreen's parents took in boarders. But people like *that*?

He waited, hoping to hear the door open and close. For a long moment he heard nothing.

And then, above him, the bushes moved.

"Boo."

Two wild eyes glared down at him, surrounding a bulbous nose crisscrossed with veins. Andrew screamed and scrambled to his feet, stuffing his iPod and binoculars into his pocket.

The two bikers, dressed in his-and-hers studded black leather, came toward him from the other side of the bush.

The man's arms were massive. An elaborate snake wound around one of them. It was a weird design. The snake had the head of a bat, dripping venom.

"Should we have him for dinner, Frances?" the man growled. "Or dessert?"

Andrew stumbled backward. He opened his mouth, preparing to shriek bloody murder.

The front door smacked open. "Mama! Papa!" Doreen called out. "He's the one! He's the kid who gave me the black stone!"

Chapter Ten

Evie turned her Boggle cubes upside down, shook hard, then set them right-side up:

S	Y	D	W
T	F	I	E
O	N	A	Qu
L	M	V	O

Taking a quick breath, she turned over her hourglass.

She was good at this. Her brain was trained to connect the letters in all sorts of twisted combinations. Each word had to be three letters or more. Quickly she began to write:

FAINT QUAINT WAN WANT WIN WON'T LOT LOTS SLOT NOT TON WEAN DIN FONT FONTS ANT ANTS ANTSY FAWN AWL OWL OWN FOWL TOW LOW NOW STOW TOWN WIDE AID AIDE AQUA OAF OAFS LOFT LOFTS LOFTY ALONE WEAN WAIF WAFT WAFTS WIDE NIFTY EDIFY

When the sand ran out, she stopped and counted her points.

Not bad — 54.

Evie checked her watch. They had left Andrew forty-nine minutes ago. Which meant he had eleven minutes to go before the hour was up. And it took about seven minutes to drive to school.

"Evie?" Marisol called from downstairs.

"Coming! I'm just finishing some work!" Evie lied.

She would give Andrew as much wiggle room as she could.

Evie lifted the Boggle container and timer off her desk and put them back in their box.

The clue sheet from Mom was underneath. She had stapled it to the grid. Couldn't very well leave *that* in the open.

As Evie took it off the desk, her eyes landed on the last two lines of the sheet's "key"— the only instructions they hadn't figured out yet:

HIDDEN IN PLAIN SIGHT
TOP L TO BOTTOM R

She glanced quickly at the grid underneath. It really was like a big Boggle game with a huge number of combinations.

Mom knew how much Evie loved Boggle. Maybe there was something else in the grid . . .

Something hidden in plain sight.

Something that went top left to bottom right . . .

She started in the upper left-hand corner of the filled-in grid. The puzzle itself hadn't been *exactly* like Boggle. In Boggle you could wrap your words any which way you wanted. But Mom made this puzzle to go down and to the right only.

Which meant maybe the hidden clue did, too.

"Evie? It's getting late . . ." Marisol called.

And that was when Evie saw it.

She grabbed a pencil and shaded in the letters.

T	E	A	M	O	L	E
I	N	H	A	L	E	D
P	R	O	U	D	T	I
S	A	Y	S	E	S	T
I	G	N	O	R	E	D
L	E	O	H	I	V	E
O	D	D	S	K	E	N

Teahouse seven? Teahouses even? It could also be tin house seven.

None of it made sense.

Evie folded up the papers, put them in her pocket, and ran downstairs. "I'm ready."

Marisol already had put on her windbreaker. "Let's book. We don't want your poor brother to be waiting for us all alone."

Yeah, poor Andrew, Evie thought. He was in deep doo-doo if he hadn't returned from his secret mission.

As they walked out to the car, Evie mulled over her puzzle solution. "Marisol?" she said, slipping into the passenger seat. "How well do you know San Francisco?"

Marisol hooked her shoulder belt and inserted the key in the ignition. "Well, I've only been here a year or so. Why?"

"Is there some kind of tin house or teahouse in the neighborhood?"

Marisol carefully backed the car out, tapping the horn gently to warn pedestrians. "There's a Japanese Teahouse in Golden Gate Park, a famous one. But it's not in the neighborhood . . ."

Evie sat up. "Golden Gate Park? Really? Could you take us there?"

"Of course," Marisol said with a gentle laugh. She was nearly to the sidewalk now.

VRRROOOOOMM!

A sudden roar sounded behind them.

"What the —?" Marisol slammed on the brakes. The car lurched to a stop.

Two motorcycles pulled up behind them, inches behind Marisol's Beetle.

Muttering an oath, Marisol pushed open the driver door and jumped out. "What kind of idiotic stunt was that?" she shouted. "You do that again and those bikes will be scrap metal, buster!"

Evie was impressed, big-time. Marisol was a lot tougher than she looked.

A huge Jabba-the-Hut of a man dismounted from his bike. His scraggly beard was stiff from the wind. "So sorry," he said. "Entirely my fault. I was just returning the intrepid young explorer."

Behind him on the seat, no longer hidden by the man's girth, was Andrew.

Chapter Eleven

"Andrew?" Marisol said, blinking uncomprehendingly at him seated on the motorbike. "You said you were staying after for math help . . ."

"We found him lurking in front of my house," Mrs. Franklin said to Marisol with a chuckle. "But I confess that as the parents of an attractive thirteen-year-old girl, we've come to expect the odd workings of young love."

Andrew looked aghast. "Young love? Doreen? *No way*! I mean, I can explain! See, I realized it was the wrong day for math help. My teacher, Ms. Plympton, didn't show up. I thought: oops, my bad. Or was it *her* bad? That was the question. Anyway, there I was in the front lobby, preparing to call home, when suddenly I thought, what if Ms. Plympton had been abducted? And so I devised a strategy —"

This was painful to watch.

"It's my fault," Evie interrupted, climbing out of the car. "I told Andrew the wrong day for after-school math help. It's Tuesday, not Friday. I got mixed up from our old school's schedule."

"Right! Tuesday!" Andrew shot back, his eyes screaming *thank you*.

"Well, thanks for getting him home safely," Marisol said to the Franklins, who tipped their black-leather caps and roared away. "And as for you," she said to Andrew, "you'd better explain why you didn't call."

As the noise died down, Andrew murmured to Marisol, "I'm seriously *not* in love with Doreen. I just got curious because I thought she was talking about me . . ."

"He gets carried away sometimes," Evie explained.

Marisol's glare softened. "Look, I know what you're going through. I moved a lot when I was a kid. At age ten I took a New York City subway to the end of the line and found myself alone on a beach at midnight. I was lonely and confused. I did strange things that made people mad. Transitions to new places are hard — dangerous, even. That's why your dad's worried. And that's why I'm here — to help you." She paused and looked at each of the twins. "But you've got to let me help."

Andrew nodded. So did Evie.

"Now, if your dad hears about this, he's going to be pretty angry. And I don't want to get you in more trouble when you've already been grounded. So let's make a deal — from now on, you come home right after school, and *I'll* help you with your math homework. I'm getting my degree in math."

"Can you do algebra?" Andrew asked.

"Algebra, calculus, game theory, cryptography — you name it," Marisol said. "Hey, I might even be able to teach your teacher a thing or two. Now, come on, let's move this car back in the garage and get cracking."

Evie shot her brother a glance. Cryptography meant code breaking.

Marisol might be useful after all.

Andrew and Evie were on their best behavior the next day. That evening Marisol took them on a drive. As they wound along the University of San Francisco campus, the cool evening wind smelled faintly of oranges and a strange, cinnamonlike scent. Just ahead, they could see the trees of Golden Gate Park.

Teahouse seven.

Evie had figured it meant the Japanese Teahouse at seven o'clock. And she'd managed to convince Marisol to take her and Andrew on a sightseeing trip. Pop was working late tonight, which was no great surprise.

Andrew sat slumped in the seat, his arms folded. After Mr. Franklin had brought him home, Andrew hadn't wanted to talk about his trip to Doreen's house very much. Except to say that it was an utter failure, and that Doreen had the most unlikely parents anyone could imagine. And to say that he didn't trust Marisol and definitely, *definitely* wouldn't go to the park with her and Evie.

Too bad. Because Evie wasn't about to pass up a chance to follow Mom's latest clue. And where Marisol and Evie went, Andrew had to go, too.

Marisol steered the car toward the park and drove west on Fulton, into the setting sun. She pulled into a space on Tenth Street, and they all piled out of the car.

Evie loved the feel of Golden Gate Park. The moment you went inside, you forgot you were in a city. The trees, tall and thick, were nothing like the scrawny things that lined the sidewalks. They cast long shadows, the sun dappling the road through the leaves as Evie, Andrew, and Marisol strolled along.

Evie reminded herself that someday, when this was all over, she'd have to return here with Mom.

They entered the grounds of the Japanese Teahouse through an ornate gate that led to a path shaded by maples. Marisol showed them a sloping Zen garden surrounded by low, sculpted pines, and a bright red pagoda with five flaring roofs. They crossed a long, wooden bridge and found themselves descending gentle steps to a cozy wooden teahouse embraced by flowering vines and overlooking a pond.

"I could live here," Evie said.

"Do they have desserts?" Andrew asked.

"Behave," said Evie.

The tables were packed, and a hostess told them there was a five-minute wait.

Andrew groaned and set off toward a small red bridge shaped like a half-circle arching upward out of the ground. Marisol followed him uneasily with her eyes.

"Leave him," Evie said with a shrug. "He's just grouchy and embarrassed about yesterday."

She glanced back into the teahouse. None of the customers seemed anxious to leave. Evie checked her watch. It was 6:51.

Teahouse seven.

What could Mom have meant?

Was she going to meet them there at seven? Were they going to get some kind of signal from a secret associate — someone like Mrs. Digitalis?

Evie eyed Marisol. What about her? Was *she* secretly in cahoots with Mom?

Evie didn't mind spying on people. And she actually liked cracking codes. It was the secrecy that bugged her.

"Jasmine tea, table three!" a waitress called to another as she walked briskly by.

"Table nine cleared," another waitress said to the hostess.

On the hostess's stand, Evie could see a laminated map of the teahouse, each table numbered and written on with marker.

And another possibility suddenly hit her. Teahouse seven could mean . . .

"Excuse me!" she called out to the hostess. "Can you seat us at table *seven*?"

The hostess craned her neck, looking toward the back of the room. "Sure. It'll just be a few minutes."

Marisol cocked her head curiously. "You know the table numbers?"

"I checked out the map," Evie said. "It . . . has a nice view."

In a few minutes the hostess was leading them through the teahouse to a small table by a window. Evie looked around for Andrew. She could see the semi-circular bridge, but he wasn't there.

"I'll try to find your brother," Marisol said, hurrying off. "He wouldn't want to miss dessert."

Evie sat down by a window that looked over a dark, thick-leafed hedge. A flowery scent wafted in, and she sat back, her arm resting on the sill.

At first she didn't notice the tiny slip of green paper stuck in the hedge. It blended with the leaves. She assumed it was someone's litter until she saw the small marks, written in white.

11 11 11

Evie's heart jumped. *The eleventh day of the eleventh month, on Andrew and Evie's eleventh birthday.* The day Mom had vanished.

She looked left and right. Marisol was gone. The waitresses were off tending other tables.

She reached out and plucked the paper off the hedge. It was actually plastic, sturdy, and attached to a green string, which in turn was attached like a fishing rod to something deeper in the hedge.

An envelope. Also green.

With writing on it:

Letters inside

Evie's hands shook. She closed her eyes, willing her heart to slow down. Clumsily she slipped her thumb under the envelope's flap and lifted it open.

She didn't know what she'd expected, but it wasn't this.

"What's that — fan mail?"

At the sound of Marisol's voice, Evie looked up with a start. "Nothing," she said, hiding the paper under the table.

Marisol smiled and sat down. "In case you were wondering, I found your brother, and he's washing his hands in the rest room."

Evie felt awful hiding the letter under the table. Guilty. Marisol had been very patient and friendly to them. She could've told Pop about Andrew sneaking off after school, but she hadn't. She'd been nothing but nice to Andrew and Evie. And how had they treated her? Rudely. Tricking her. Running off to spy and getting caught by biker parents.

It wasn't *her* fault that she had to tail Andrew and Evie. She was just a college student.

A very smart college student. With knowledge of cryptography.

Evie fingered the new code nervously. Marisol might be able to help. But Mom had been very clear: No telling anyone about her messages. No mentioning to a soul that she was trying to contact them.

Marisol could tell something was up. Evie knew it. But Evie also knew that a word game, to any other unsuspecting person, was just a word game. It could have come from anywhere — a classmate, a newspaper, the Web. There was no need to explain its *real* origin, was there?

"Actually, it's a kind of puzzle," Evie said, bringing the paper up to the table. "A hobby of mine. A word game . . ."

Just up a winding path from the teahouse, Andrew emerged from the rest room. He glanced in both directions and hurried to his right, toward the gift shop. If he was quick, they wouldn't miss him.

Marisol was nice, but she made him uncomfortable. Maybe it was just bad feelings left over from when he'd thought she was Pop's girlfriend. Maybe it was just the fact that he'd been caught red-handed by the Franklins and been humiliated in front of her.

Whatever. He'd wanted to get away from her and Evie. And now he was glad he had. Because if he'd stayed in the teahouse, he wouldn't have seen the gardener.

And the gardener was definitely not what he appeared to be.

There he was now — emerging from a door, carrying a rake. He was wearing sunglasses, a windbreaker with the collar turned up, and a floppy hat. His back was to Andrew, his face hidden.

Andrew crouched behind a hedge. He took out his binoculars and trained them on the man's head, hoping he'd turn.

The man lumbered from side to side when he walked. He looked like he would pulverize any flower bed he came near.

When he finally did turn, Andrew saw the scraggly gray beard. And the roundish, red nose.

It was the man who'd made him miserable last night. Who'd sneaked up behind him and traumatized him for life.

Doreen's dad. Mr. Franklin. No doubt about it.

What was he doing here? Was this his *job*? Hell's Angel by day, Zen gardener by night?

Mr. Franklin nodded to a couple passing by. Then, after they were gone, he reached into his pocket and pulled out a small coin.

No, not a coin. It was white, not silver.

The man moved quickly for his size. Andrew lost him as he ducked around the other side of the teahouse. The side that Marisol and Evie were on.

Andrew tiptoed to the edge of the building and peered around.

At first he didn't see the man. But he did see the hedge move ever so slightly under the window where Evie sat.

A hand appeared over the top of the hedge. Silently it placed the white disk on the underside of the window. Then it disappeared.

Chapter Twelve

A bugging device.

Doreen's dad was a spy, and he was listening in on Evie's conversation.

Why?

How could it be?

It made no sense, but there it was.

Andrew ran back the way he came, around the other side of the teahouse, keeping close to the hedges and vines and trees, just in case.

As he came around to the entrance, he spotted Mr. Franklin rushing away. He was wearing earphones now. The rake was gone.

Andrew raced into the teahouse. He could see Marisol and Evie hunched over a sheet of paper.

Standing close to the entrance, he caught Evie's attention, gesturing wildly for her to leave. *COME HERE*, he mouthed.

Evie folded up the paper and put it in her pocket. Andrew heard her mutter something about "defective mental capacity" to Marisol as she reluctantly headed toward Andrew.

"Andrew, I found a clue from Mom," Evie said.

"SSSSHHHH!"

"*What is wrong with you?*"

"You're being bugged!" Andrew whispered. "I saw him put the bug under your window."

"Who?"

"Doreen's dad!"

"You *are* crazy."

"No! He's disguised as a gardener. He's a spy."

Andrew led her out of the teahouse and around to the side, pointing to the white disk. Evie followed, her eyes narrowed. "You're right," she whispered. "What's he trying to hear?"

"You!" Andrew said. "And maybe Marisol. Who is Marisol, anyway?"

"She's a college student, Andrew! Come on, pick your battles. You can't suspect *everyone*!"

Marisol did a double take when she saw the twins. "Where are you going?" she called from the open window.

Evie pointed to her watch. Time to go, she mouthed.

"But we haven't had our tea yet!" Marisol shouted.

Evie put her fingers to her lips and gestured urgently for Marisol to come.

Minutes later they were heading out of the park. Marisol looked flustered. "I don't know what you two are up to."

"It's late," Evie said.

"For tea and cookies?" Marisol said. "*You* were the ones who wanted to come here."

"I have a lot of homework," Andrew said.

Marisol gave him a look. It was a lame excuse. He knew it.

Marisol picked up the pace. She didn't utter a word to them as they got into the car and drove home.

"We should say something to her," Evie whispered to him in the backseat. "About the bug."

"We're not supposed to tell anyone we're spies," Andrew replied.

"Not the whole story — just *something*, so we don't seem rude."

Marisol jammed on the brakes at a red light — a little too hard. Her eyes blazed at them in the rearview mirror. "Look," she said, "I know you resent having a babysitter. And I don't blame you. You're on the old side to have one. But you're also old enough to know about the feelings of other people — to understand that it is rude to whisper behind backs and change plans without explanation."

Andrew felt awful. Marisol didn't understand. She *couldn't* understand. Of course her feelings were hurt. But what could they do?

"Sorry," Evie said. "It's just that . . . well, we're involved in a special training program . . . for kids. Something related to the military. We can't explain more than that. That code we found? We're not supposed to handle it in public, that's why we have to go."

"It's part of the rules," Andrew chimed in.

The light turned green. Marisol's eyes went back to the road. "That's fair," she said as the car moved on. "Thanks for explaining. I was a military brat, too — and I'm pretty good at word puzzles myself, you know. Maybe, if you want, I can help you."

Evie glanced at Andrew. He shrugged his shoulders. "Yeah, that'd be great," Evie said.

Pop wasn't home when they arrived. Evie, Andrew, and Marisol ran upstairs and gathered around Evie's desk as she spread out the sheet and envelope from the teahouse.

Andrew's feelings about Marisol were starting to soften. She wasn't too awful, for a college kid. She knew about codes. She didn't ask too many questions. She believed Evie's story about the training program. How bad could she be? Plus, now that they knew Doreen's parents were after Mom, he and Evie needed all the help they could get to find her first.

"Let's see . . ." Marisol said. "The envelope says 'Letters inside' — but there's only one letter. That's a clue. She's not talking about a letter as in *message*. She's talking about *letters* as in A, B, C."

"She?" Evie asked. "What make you think it's a *she*?"

"I'm just assuming. Girls are smarter." Marisol winked at Andrew. "The problem is, there are pictures inside the envelope — pictures of *things*, not letters."

She was good, Andrew thought. Very good. "Maybe the first letter of each forms a word."

Evie wrote the names of each thing next to the drawing. "An envelope . . ." she said. "A city skyline . . . a snail . . . a guitar . . . an eagle . . . a ballet dancer . . . a candy bar . . . a restaurant menu."

"If we take the first letters," Andrew said, "that's E, C, S, G, E, B, C, and R. I'll run that through my anagram program!"

"Seven consonants and two E's?" Evie said. "I don't think so."

"Good point," Andrew replied. "It must be something else."

"What if it's not the *first* letters?" Marisol asked. "After all, it says, 'Letters *inside*.'"

"Letters inside *envelope*," Andrew said, "*guitar . . . eagle . . . menu . . .*"

"That's it!" Evie exclaimed.

"That's what?" Andrew said.

"Say these aloud. They have something in common. Letters inside — or syllables that sound like letters. Envelope has an N. City has a T. Guitar has an R."

"Snail?" Andrew said.

Marisol pointed to the beret. "Look what he's wearing. He's a *French* snail. An escargot! The letter *S*."

"Oui," Evie said. She began filling in the list:

	ENVELOPE ("N"-VELOPE)	N
	CITY (CI-"T")	T
	ESCARGOT ("S"-CARGOT)	S
	GUITAR (GUIT-"R")	R

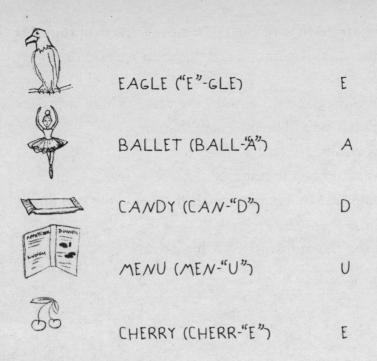

EAGLE ("E"-GLE)	E
BALLET (BALL-"A")	A
CANDY (CAN-"D")	D
MENU (MEN-"U")	U
CHERRY (CHERR-"E")	E

"Run *that* through your anagram program," Evie declared.

"Just a minute." Marisol was scribbling on another sheet, line after line of rearranged letters. "I think I know what it is . . ."

She held up her sheet. Across the bottom were written the words SEE TUNDRA. "There's a traveling exhibit at the Academy of Sciences Natural History Museum," she said. "It's all about the Siberian tundra."

"Excellent!" Evie stood up from her desk. "Let's go."

"I'm afraid they're closed by now," Marisol said. "Is this some sort of game? Like you find a prize or something?"

Andrew looked down into the crate. There was only one item left now. The old metal handle.

This was it.

This could be the last clue.

Whatever Mom meant for them, they'd have to find it now.

"Yeah," he said softly. "A big prize."

Chapter Thirteen

"Do you have that metal handle?" Evie asked. "That thing from the crate?"

"Yes, I have it," Andrew shot back, walking across the parking lot of the Academy of Arts and Sciences Natural History Museum. "That's the hundredth time you've asked."

He was grumpier than usual today, but Evie didn't blame him. She wasn't feeling too jolly herself. Someone was after them, and that somebody was the father of the girl who had stolen the school election. The girl who had the black stone Mom had given them.

She and Andrew had done the worst possible thing. Misinterpreted a clue — "nevus mole" — and possibly given up Mom to her enemy.

It seemed too bizarre — too coincidental — to be true. But if there was one thing they'd learned in Connecticut, it was that nothing could ever be assumed. What could *nevus mole* have really meant? Did it matter anymore?

One thing was sure — they were *not* going to misinterpret anything again.

The academy was in a temporary building on Howard Street, way on the other side of town from its usual home in Golden Gate Park. Marisol had managed to get them there just after the place opened at 10 A.M.

Pop had seemed pleased about the trip. Probably because this morning was the first time Andrew and Evie hadn't complained about Marisol. Of course, none of them had mentioned *why* they were going. Any mention of code solving would be risky. Pop was a covert-military-operations guy. He'd be suspicious.

They made their way through the museum to the tundra exhibit. Andrew stared wide-eyed at the dioramas and stuffed animals. "Did you know that the Siberian tiger can grow to nine feet long?"

"Do you see what you came for?" Marisol said.

Evie's eyes darted around the room, taking in the security guard who had a rolled-up sheet of paper in her hand. The twenty-something man who seemed a little too nervous. The rumpled paper on the floor that was, on closer inspection, only a candy wrapper. "Not yet," she said. "I'm not even sure what I'm looking for."

"Well, we do have time," Marisol replied, checking her watch. "Your dad's already at CHQ by now, and he's not likely to come home before dark. I must confess, though, the mineral and gems exhibit is more up my alley. You guys won't disappear if I check it out for a few minutes?"

"CHQ?" Evie said.

Marisol nodded. "He was called in to work at the last minute."

"In Verkhoyansk, temperatures go from ninety-three degrees Fahrenheit in the summer to *minus* ninety-three in the winter!" Andrew called out.

Evie smiled. "We'll be here awhile."

As she watched Marisol slip away, she had an uncomfortable feeling.

CHQ?

That meant "Company Headquarters." Pop *never* mentioned that name to anybody. Only rarely had he ever used it in front of Andrew and Evie. And, of course, Mom.

Pop was slipping. Or maybe not. Maybe he really *was* interested in Marisol.

Distractedly, Evie went from display to display. She learned all there was to know about permafrost, the snowy owl, the Trans-Siberian Railroad, and oil drilling in Yakutsk. Twice she made eye contact with the security guard, who smiled and said nothing. Three times she rescued sheets of paper wedged in odd places — all programs and brochures.

"This isn't working," she finally said to Andrew. "Maybe we didn't decode the clue right."

Andrew shrugged. "We could try again. Where's Marisol?"

"Admiring the rocks and minerals. Let's find her."

They made their way through the museum to the mineral exhibit and glanced around the jade boulders, but Marisol wasn't there. They checked the African Room, the Far Side Gallery. Eventually they wound their way through the whole place. No luck.

Andrew and Evie finally ended up in the parking lot. Many more cars were parked than before. Having memorized the location, Evie confidently led Andrew to the space.

But another car was in it.

"What the —?" Evie said. "She's gone."

"An emergency," Andrew suggested. "Or an errand. She'll be back. Let's get some lunch."

Evie didn't like this. Not at all.

Marisol was a little more mysterious than she wanted her to be.

"Andrew . . . how did Marisol know about CHQ? Do you think Pop told her?"

"He's slipping," Andrew said with a shrug. "Either that or *recruiting*. I mean, Marisol is the kind of person the Company likes to hire. She's really smart. She's in college."

"Do we *know* that? Have we seen her carrying any books? Has she talked about her professors and classes and extracurricular activities? Has she shown us a student ID?"

"No. But so what?"

"It just doesn't add up, Andrew. She knows about CHQ. She solves clues like the best of them. When we got back from the teahouse, Marisol should have had no idea who wrote those picture clues — but she used the word *she*. As if she *knew* Mom had done it."

"So you think Marisol is a bad guy?" Andrew thought a moment. "Maybe she's on Mom's side, like Mrs. Digitalis. Maybe she's been sent to help us. I mean, she brought us here. And face it, if it weren't for her, we wouldn't have solved the code."

Andrew had a point.

Or did he?

Evie took out the code sheet and looked at the letters — N, T, S, R, E, A, D, U, E. Lots of vowels. Lots of popular consonants.

"How do we know she solved it correctly?" Evie asked.

Andrew glanced over her shoulder. "Stun a deer," he said.

"True sedan," Evie said.

"Eat red sun. Actually, it could be a lot of different combinations. Do you think we got the wrong one?"

"I think we were tricked."

"But what *is* the right one? Mom isn't usually so vague!"

One clue remaining.

One item from the crate.

Mom wouldn't let them get this close and then let them down. She was a pro.

She was never vague.

"Where's the handle, Andrew?" Evie said. "The last thing in the crate?"

Andrew unhooked his pack and dug out the handle. Together they examined it, reading what was stamped into the metal.

Property of SFCCM

817543962

"SF is San Francisco . . ." Andrew said. "And CCM . . . ?"

"I don't know. But it looks like something from some old-fashioned vehicle —"

"That's it! From a cable car. San Francisco Cable Car . . . M!"

Evie pulled out her cell phone and tapped 411. "Information? Hi, I'd like the address of the Cable Car Museum . . ."

Chapter Fourteen

CLANG! CLANG!

The cable car was climbing. Andrew tried to keep the sheet of paper steady on his lap, but as they passed Union Square the street rose up all the way to Washington Street. It was hard to write.

Andrew copied the numbers carefully onto the sheet — 817543962. Did they mean anything?

Not enough digits for a phone number.

He held the handle close. The words and numbers had been etched in the metal crudely, as if by hand. He wouldn't have expected that of a museum. A regular person with some kind of metal stamper, yes. Did that mean Mom had stamped it in? Maybe. Or maybe this handle was made in the olden days, when everything was cruder.

The conductor rang a big, old-fashioned bell in a jazzy rhythm as the car approached the crest of the hill. Cars, which didn't drive on the tracks, were jammed on either side, bumper to bumper. This side of the hill, with the park and the shops and the theaters, was a great tourist attraction.

Andrew was deep in thought, trying to connect the numbers somehow to Mom's drawings, when Evie nearly knocked him off his seat. "There she is!" she cried out, pointing out onto the street.

Marisol's car was just ahead, near the top of the hill, stuck at a red light at the intersection of California Street.

"Where is she going?" Andrew asked.

"The same place *we're* going, I'll bet." Evie ducked down, pulling on Andrew's arm. "Don't let her see us!"

He fell off his seat onto the floor, the metal handle clanking beside him. As the car rolled across California, he raised his head high enough to see Marisol's car. She was wearing sunglasses that covered most of her face, but the impatient expression was unmistakable.

"How did she know?" Andrew asked.

"Because she's a spy, not a college student," Evie hissed. "She gave us the wrong solution to Mom's clues, then dumped us at the museum to get rid of us while *she* went to the right place. But she sure didn't count on this traffic!"

Andrew hated the sound of this. "What's she going to do there?"

"We'll soon find out," Evie said.

The cable car rolled to a stop at Washington Street. On the side of the street where the hill began its downward slope rose the arched windows of the Cable Car Muscum, which was also the control center for the cable car system.

Andrew hopped off. Marisol was still a block or so behind.

He and Evie ran into the building, where they were greeted by a bronze plaque that said SHEAVE ROOM VIEWING AREA DOWNSTAIRS TO THE LEFT.

They descended a staircase past a window that showed a set of underground pulleys turning a thick metal cable. "*That's* what pulls the cars?" Andrew said, stopping to watch.

"Come on!" Evie yanked him downward. A low humming noise grew into a deep mechanical rumble as they emerged into a cavernous room, about a block long, that vaulted upward past street level.

At either end of the room were massive sets of wheels at least two stories high. They turned together, synchronized, moving tightly strung lengths of cable that continued out past the building walls and under the street. The area was surrounded by a sturdy metal fence covered by a wood railing. To the side was an exhibit area with plaques, displays, viewing stations, old paintings, photos, models, and actual vintage cable cars.

It was awesome. But Marisol would be trying to park about now, and Evie was already seeking out a museum official. There would be time for sightseeing later.

"Excuse me, sir," Evie said to a jolly-looking older man in a train-conductor suit. "My brother found something that may belong to the museum. We were wondering what it was."

Andrew handed over the metal grip to the man, who looked at it through glasses perched at the end of his nose. "Looks like ours, all right . . ." he said. "In fact, one of our museum cars *is* missing a grip handle. This 'SFCCM,' though . . . it's odd. We never engrave our parts like that."

Andrew's pulse raced. The grip was the end of the line. He would return it to its rightful place and then . . . what?

What was Mom sending them here for?

"Which car is missing the handle?" he asked. "I'll return it."

The old man handed the gizmo back to Andrew. "Grip car 27," he said. "Built in 1878, I believe."

He gestured to a wooden car, polished to a high shine,

with a running board and totally open sides. Its seats faced outward on the sides, leaving a long space down the middle for the driver.

Andrew smiled at his sister. "This is it."

"She's coming," Evie whispered back.

Andrew looked over his shoulder. He saw Marisol's legs descending from the stairway landing.

"Go," Evie said. "I'll take care of her."

Andrew rushed over to the grip car. Its handle had been replaced.

What was he supposed to do now? Take off the replacement and put the old one back? Look for another car with another stolen handle?

Something was missing, still. Some bit of knowledge. Some guidance.

He realized he still didn't know the real answer to the word puzzle. It wasn't SEE TUNDRA — but what *was* it?

Andrew pulled out the clue sheet.

Across the room, Evie approached Marisol. The babysitter's eyes darted around the room. She looked beleaguered and anxious.

Traitor, Evie thought. *Sneak.*

"Hi," Evie called out.

For a moment Marisol's face went blank, as if she didn't know who Evie was — or couldn't believe she was there.

"Oh my Lord, you're all right!" she finally cried out, wrapping Evie in a hug. "I was so worried. I *hoped* I'd find you here! Where were you?"

"Where were *you*?" Evie asked. "We went looking in the mineral room —"

"You did? I went back to the tundra exhibit! We must have crossed paths. Well, I figured you got bored and went out to the car — but when I didn't see you there, I just panicked. I remembered Andrew said he liked the Cable Car Museum, so I came here, but I got stuck in traffic! I'm soooo sorry. Where is he?"

Evie's resolve wavered. Marisol's eyes were glassy, brimming with tears. She was glancing around the room now, trying to find Andrew among the handful of tourists wandering through the exhibit.

Evie had to test her.

"He found out the secret," she lied. "The real meaning of the coded pictures. He unscrambled the letters."

There.

Evie saw it. It was a momentary shift of facial muscles, not even a twitch. A shadow of some comprehension that passed across Marisol's face like the flicker of a mothwing.

"And . . . what was that meaning?" Marisol asked.

She was composed now, her face open and curious. Too open and calm for a babysitter was had nearly lost her charges.

"You're a spy, aren't you?" Evie said.

"A *what*?" Marisol shot back.

"You gave us the wrong answer on purpose. You left us at the museum. Maybe you meant to duck out quickly and come back, thinking we wouldn't notice. But it was a dumb idea. You got stuck in traffic. And now you're too late. Because you knew something we didn't know. You're after my mom and you knew she meant for us to come here — and now we've gotten here first and spoiled your plans."

Marisol leaned against an exhibit stand, rubbing her eyes. "How stupid I am. How totally stupid . . ."

Evie looked nervously over her shoulder. Behind her the machinery thrummed, but she couldn't see Andrew on either side of the sheaves.

"Okay, Evie," Marisol said with a sigh, "you're right. I am a spy. I'm an employee of the Company. But you've misunderstood the whole thing. I was sent to keep an eye on you. To protect you."

"Hard to do that from here if we're halfway across town, at the other museum."

"I couldn't let you come here. It was too dangerous. I'm not at liberty to tell you why. But I do need that metal handle . . ."

Marisol was walking toward Evie now.

Slowly.

Evie took an involuntary step back.

The handle? How did she know about that? Had Andrew shown it to her? He couldn't have.

"I — I'm not at liberty to tell you," Evie said.

Marisol's expression tightened. "This is not about you, young lady," she said, moving closer . . . closer. "Come on. *Where is it?*"

Evie felt her back make contact with the railing. She could feel the vibration of the sheave motors. Below her the ground fell off to where the wheels turned with unyielding strength, pulling the cables taut between their grooves.

Marisol was eye to eye with her now.

"I'll scream," Evie said.

"I'll push," Marisol whispered.

"*Evie!*"

Andrew's voice echoed through the room. He was running toward a vintage cable car, holding the handle aloft. "Oh, hi, Marisol! Hey, Evie, I've checked them all. The guy was wrong. There's only one car left, and I think this is it! Whatever Mom wanted us to find — it's in here!"

Marisol leaped across the room with the reflexes of a sprinter.

"ANDREW, SHE'S A SPY!" Evie screamed. "SHE'S WORKING AGAINST MOM!"

Andrew stopped in his tracks. "Huh?"

Marisol plowed into him, snatching the handle away. Andrew fell hard to the floor, banging against the running board of a cable car.

Museum visitors were scattering, running toward the exit.

"Excuse me!" a guard shouted, running toward Marisol. "You can't —"

Evie sprang toward the cable car. She could see the grip lever now, and Andrew was right. It was missing a handle. It was the one.

Marisol was inside, crouching by the conductor's seat. She lifted it open, reached in, and pulled out a small black electronic device.

"Ma'am," the guard said, "I'm afraid I'm going to have to ask you to leave."

"Absolutely," Marisol replied. "I am out of here. These kids, sir, were hiding something that belongs to me. A personal tracker. State of the art." She dusted herself off and began sauntering backward, toward the stairs, as the guard followed warily. "If you know the right coordinates," she said, "you can find anyone in the world. Even someone no one seems to be able to locate. You see, that person *wants* to be located — and that's why she hid it here."

The guard stared, slack-jawed and silent.

Evie lunged forward, but Marisol quickly put the device in her pocket and headed to the exit.

"I'll say hi to your mom for you," she said over her shoulder, and then took the stairs two at a time.

Chapter Fifteen

Evie bolted for the stairs. She expected Andrew to be behind her, but he was still on the floor.

"*Why are you just sitting there?*" she shouted, racing after Marisol. She was at the top landing now. Plowing through tourists like a linebacker.

Evie tried to dart around a man the size of an SUV, but he darted into her path and she fell down.

As she scrambled to her feet, Andrew ran past her. Finally off his behind.

Outside, passing engines roared. Traffic had cleared. Marisol would be out of here fast.

Evie and Andrew reached the ground floor at the same time. Two guards had hold of Marisol now, but she was quick and slippery, ducking out of their grip and sprinting for the door.

Evie started after her, but Andrew grabbed her tightly by the arm.

"*What are you doing?*" she shouted.

Marisol was almost out of the museum. As she

reached the door, two people pushed it open from outside. They stopped, standing shoulder to shoulder, blocking the exit.

Evie couldn't believe her eyes.

It was Mr. and Mrs. Franklin.

"*GET HER!*" Evie shouted, running to help.

"No!" Andrew said, waving something overhead. "Let her go!"

Mr. and Mrs. Franklin looked at him — giving Marisol just enough time to escape.

Just like that, she was gone.

Out into the street.

The two big lugs were still standing there. Like overgrown fire hydrants.

"Move!" Evie struggled to get past them but they wouldn't move. "MOVE!"

They were smiling.

Smiling!

They didn't know.

Marisol had escaped with the one device that would have allowed Andrew and Evie to find their mom. The thing she'd tried to protect behind such an elaborate scheme — clues to other clues, scavenger hunts. A plan so spidery and complex that it couldn't possibly be cracked by anyone.

A plan that had gone up in smoke, because of Andrew's big mouth.

"Your brother has something to show you, dear," Mrs. Franklin said.

Evie spun around.

With a sheepish grin, Andrew held out a small, black electronic box. Etched into the casing was the word ONYX — and around the logo was a silver, serpentine logo.

A snake. With a head of a bat.

"Isn't that . . . ?" Evie said.

Mr. Franklin rolled up his sleeve to show his tattoo. A couple of tourists oohed, and he turned red.

"Then what did Marisol take?" Evie stammered.

Andrew sighed sadly. "Remember my Star Raiders Intergalactic Cell Communicator?"

Evie's jaw dropped. She threw her arms around her brother.

Sometimes — *sometimes* — he was smarter than she was.

Two police officers burst through the door, their walkie-talkies blaring. "Everything all right?" they asked Mr. Franklin.

"Totally under control, Bill," Doreen's father replied,

looking around the room at a crowd of baffled, frozen faces. "But, er, I think we'd all better leave these gentle people in peace."

He held open the door.

Evie was numb as she walked through. "You found the device yourself!" she said as they emerged on Powell Street. "How did you do it?"

"When you were talking to Marisol," Andrew replied, "I figured out what Mom had meant. Those numbers on the grip handle — eight-one-seven-five-four-three-nine-six-two — they were the numbers one to nine, rearranged. And there were nine letters that answered Mom's clues. So I put those letters in the same order. Eight for the eighth clue, one for the first clue, and so on. And the answer wasn't SEE TUNDRA at all!"

He took the sheet from his pocket and showed Evie:

	ENVELOPE ("N"-VELOPE)	N
	CITY (CI-"T")	T
	ESCARGOT ("S"-CARGOT)	S
	GUITAR (GUIT-"R")	R

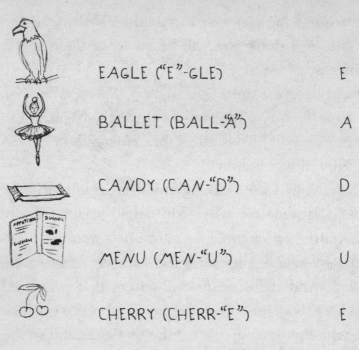

EAGLE ("E"-GLE)   E

BALLET (BALL-"A")   A

CANDY (CAN-"D")   D

MENU (MEN-"U")   U

CHERRY (CHERR-"E")   E

81754 3962 =
UNDERSEAT

"*You* figured this out?" Evie said.

"I'm not as stupid as I look," Andrew replied.

Mr. Franklin, who had come out of the building behind them, chuckled. "I had a big sister who was just like that."

"I found the cable car with the missing handle right away," Andrew said, "and sure enough, the device was there. I was just going to take it and leave. But then I saw you and Marisol. I had a bad feeling about that, so I went with my instinct. I decided to trick her so we could get away safely. Out came the real tracking device. In went the fake — my Intergalactic Cell Communicator! And so Marisol is in her car right now, at a red light, wondering why her fancy tracker is saying 'Warning, warning, plasma beam attack in Quadrant Four!' "

The vision was priceless. Evie had to steady herself against the red-brick wall of the museum as she burst out laughing.

"So . . . Mr. and Mrs. Franklin — you work with Mom?" Andrew asked.

Mrs. Franklin shook her head. "We just know *of* her. There's a small network of us across the country. We don't know each other's names, but we're in constant touch. Just before you moved, we received a call —"

"From a nice old lady who sounds like a gardener?" Evie asked.

"Could be," Mrs. Franklin said. "She told us you were here, and that some other network operatives were planting clues for you, under your mom's instructions. As for us, we weren't to do a thing until we received the onyx from Doreen. That was all Doreen knew — if someone gave her the onyx, she was to give it to us and tell us who you were. Then we were to look after you."

Mr. Franklin blushed. "That's my code name. Onyx. It *was* Ox, but I had it changed."

"Even so, we were nervous about your IDs," his wife said, "so we asked her to bring us a handwriting sample. She tried. But you know Doreen. She made this elaborate plan to create a distraction during lunch, just after you cast your vote — and then she'd find your ballots and bring them to us."

Evie cringed. Doreen hadn't tried to rig the elections after all.

"But I saw you in Golden Gate Park, Mr. Franklin, with a bugging device!"

"There goes my vaunted skill at disguise," Mr. Franklin replied. "See, we didn't know anything about Marisol, but we were suspicious. I was collecting data."

Marisol had almost ruined it, Evie realized. But she was gone now. She hadn't blocked them from Mom. And now she wouldn't be able to find Mom herself. "So can we find our mother now? We're finally that close?"

Mr. Franklin gently took the device from Andrew. "Soon," he said. "Very soon. The tracker is still in beta. The biometric coordinates necessary for personal ID are very tricky. It's something I've been contracted to do. Unfortunately, we don't yet have the right ones for your mom. Our instructions were to protect you until you found the device. Now we must take the next steps. Immediately."

He backed away, punching numbers into a keypad.

"We won't stop until we find her," Mrs. Franklin said, "at no small risk to our own lives — but hey, that's what we signed on for. And then, when we find her, we hope it'll be possible to rescue her right away. We will stay in contact with you the whole time until she's home again. But it may not be easy. And it may take a long time. The people who want her are very, very skillful . . ."

Her voice trailed off, and her face grew sad as she turned to look up the block.

Evie and Andrew followed her glance.

Mr. Franklin and his motorcycle were gone.

By the look on Mrs. Franklin's face, she wasn't expecting him back anytime soon.

Epilogue

"Before the final bell, I have an announcement to make!" Ms. Skinner's voice thundered over the school loudspeaker that Monday. *"I would like to extend my congratulations to the newly elected president of the Student Council . . . Sarah Yu!"*

A cheer went up throughout the school.

Andrew felt sad for Doreen, who was in his last-period English class. She kept a firm, stoic smile on her face as she packed her backpack. No tears. A couple of friends patted her on the back, voicing their sympathy, and she nodded.

He caught up with her in the hallway after school was over. "We know you didn't try to rig the election," he said. "I'm sorry you didn't win."

Doreen looked a little startled, but she nodded appreciatively. "I know your mom is missing. I'm sorry about that, too. I hope my dad finds her. Maybe when he comes back, she'll be with him."

Andrew didn't know what to say. They had something in common now. Maybe they could learn to become friends.

Maybe they'd have something to celebrate soon.

"Good luck," he said.

"You, too," Doreen replied, turning to leave.

Andrew leaned against the marble-tiled lobby wall as he waited for his sister. Outside, buses pulled into the circular driveway, and a few parents waited in their cars by the curb. No Marisol, of course — that was a relief. He and Evie would be able to walk home like normal twelve-year-olds.

The incident at the Cable Car Museum had passed practically unnoticed — no press coverage in a city where many more exciting things had happened that day. Andrew and Evie had debated whether to tell Pop the truth about their "nanny," but in the end decided not to. Revealing her identity as a spy would have given up too much information about Mom. So instead they'd sat uncomfortably while Pop fretted about Marisol's "unexplained disappearance." He hadn't been able to reach her by phone or e-mail on Sunday, and the college said that she'd withdrawn.

Andrew knew he should have felt relieved. In the end, the good guys had won. Mr. Franklin had the Onyx instrument and Marisol had been fooled. But it wasn't a victory at all. Marisol had discovered his and Evie's secret — that Mom was in contact with them, sending them codes. And Marisol would pass that information to the people she was working for.

Who *was* she working for? What did they want? Was Mom in danger now — because of Andrew and Evie's stupidity? Because they trusted a spy?

"Earth to Andrew," Evie said, waving her hand in front of Andrew's face. "Come on, let's walk home as free people."

Andrew shook himself back to reality and followed his sister outside. "Evie, I keep thinking we did something really dumb."

"I know, and it's my fault for showing Marisol the code," Evie replied as they headed away from the school.

"Now Mom may never contact us again. It'll be too risky."

Evie nodded. "But maybe she won't need to. Mr. Franklin is on Mom's trail. He'll find her — and that's thanks to you, little brother. You switched the tracking device. I owe you, big-time. Whatever you want, it's yours. You name it."

Andrew thought a moment. Evie didn't make offers like this very often. "Ice cream cones at Norman's, in the Cannery?"

Evie gave him a grudging look, then nodded. The twins changed direction, heading south toward Fisherman's Wharf.

Moments later, holding their cones, Andrew and Evie wandered along the small beach that lined the harbor. The sun had broken through the clouds, and Alcatraz Island stood in sharp relief out on the bay, its stark prison walls shimmering against the distant dun-colored hills of Marin County.

Evie licked her butter pecan cone carefully, keeping her distance from Andrew and his four-scoop waffle-cone extravanganza that threatened to topple into the sand at any moment. They emerged near the big "turnaround" for the Hyde Street cable car line and watched two burly men pull and push a car into the center of a huge wooden turntable, then spin it slowly around until the car was headed back the way it had come. People lined up, herded into place by iron gates. "Don't even think about it," Evie said, eyeing her brother.

Andrew swallowed a mouthful of chocolate brownie

fudge ice cream, but had to cough because the sprinkles (or maybe it was the walnuts) caught in his throat. "Not while I'm still eating," he said.

"Not even *after* you've finished eating," Evie said. "I don't want to step on a cable car ever again."

Andrew felt her hand close around his arm. He tried to pull away, but that made her yank harder. A lump of fudge, perched over the edge of the now-softening waffle cone, broke loose. Andrew tried to save it, but the entire cone cracked. His dessert hurtled downward and landed in an undignified brown lump in the sand. "You owe me another one!" Andrew blurted out.

"You pulled away."

"You grabbed my arm. I demand a re-cone!"

The cable car bell clanged, and the conductor shouted, "All aboard!"

Evie sighed. "Okay, how about we take a ride home on the cable car instead. A peace offering."

Andrew glanced at the people jockeying for seats on the car. "I thought you said you didn't want to do that."

"It's cheaper than a monster cone!"

No. Do not be tempted, Andrew told himself. This was a matter of justice. How long would it be until he'd have the opportunity for a tasty treat like this again?

Although it would be fun to ride the cable car now, especially knowing how the system worked — the cable threaded underground, winding around the network of sheaves . . .

The last person in line climbed aboard, and the car began rolling. "Andrew?" Evie said urgently.

But Andrew's knees had locked. His eye was on the front of the car. A man was getting up from his seat, pointing his camera toward the vista over the bay. He smiled to another rider, a woman who had been standing, and offered her his seat.

As the car lurched forward, across Beach Street, the woman briefly turned in Andrew's direction.

She was smiling.

And a word, caught in a choke at the edge of his throat, finally burst out as the car disappeared out of sight.

"Mom!"

"Andrew? Are you all right?" Evie asked.

"*It's Mom, Evie!*" Andrew shouted. "*Mom is on that car!*"

"Are you sure?"

"YES!"

He took off in pursuit, but the light had changed on

Beach and traffic was thick. "Andrew, don't!" Evie shouted, pulling her brother back as a taxi skidded to avoid him.

They both watched helplessly as the car rose steadily uphill, swallowed up in a swirl of cars and buses, until it was out of sight.